ALMOST NO MEMORY

L. Davis b. 1947

ALMOST NO MEMORY

[STORIES]

LYDIA DAVIS

THE ECCO PRESS

THE ECCO PRESS
100 West Broad Street
Hopewell, New Jersey 08525

Published simultaneously in Canada by
Penguin Books Canada Ltd., Ontario
Printed in the United States of America

Interior design by Cynthia Krupat
Published by arrangement with Farrar, Straus and Giroux

Library of Congress Cataloging-in-Publication Data
Davis, Lydia.
Almost no memory / Lydia Davis. — 1st Ecco ed.
p.   cm.
ISBN 0-88001-606-X
I. Title.
[PS3554.A9356A79   1998]
813'.54—dc21   97-44249
CIP

Acknowledgments appear on page 193.

9   8   7   6   5   4   3   2   1

FIRST PAPERBACK EDITION 1998

CONTENTS

ALMOST NO MEMORY

MEAT, MY HUSBAND

My husband's favorite food, in childhood, was corned beef. I found this out yesterday when friends came over and we started talking about food. At some point they asked what our favorite childhood foods had been. I couldn't think of any, but my husband didn't have to think before answering.

"Corned beef," he said.

"Corned beef with an egg on it!" one of our friends added.

My husband often ate in diners before we met. He had two he liked, but he preferred the one where they did a particularly good hot roast beef sandwich. He still likes a good piece of roast beef, or steak, or hamburger mixed with sauce and spices and grilled outdoors with brochettes of onions and peppers.

But I'm the one who cooks most of his meals now. Often I make him meals with no meat in them at all because I don't think meat is good for us. Often there is no seafood in them either, because most seafood isn't good for us either, and there is almost never any fish in them, partly because I can't remember which sorts of fish may be safe to eat and which are almost certainly not, but mainly because he likes fish only when it's served in a restaurant or cooked in such a way that he can't tell it's fish. Often there is no cheese in our meals either, because of the problem with fat. I'll make him a brown-rice casserole, for example, or winter vegetables with parsley sauce, or turnip soup with turnip greens, or white bean and eggplant gratin, or polenta with spicy vegetables.

"Why don't you make the foods I like?" he asks sometimes.

"Why don't you like the foods I make?" I answer.

Once I marinated slabs of tofu in tamari sauce, champagne vinegar, red wine, toasted marjoram, and dried Chinese mushrooms simmered in water. I marinated them for four or five days and then served them to him, sliced thin, in a sandwich with horseradish and mayonnaise, slices of red onion, lettuce and tomato. First he said the tofu was still very bland, which is what he always says about tofu, then he said that on the other hand, if he hadn't known it was there, he wouldn't have been able to taste the tofu anyway because there were so many other things in the sandwich. He said it was all right, and then he said he knew tofu was good for him.

Sometimes he likes what I make, and if he's in a good mood he says so. Once I made him a cucumber salad with feta cheese and red onion and he liked it, saying it tasted Greek. Another time I made him a lentil salad with peppers and mint and he liked that, too, though he said it tasted like dirt.

But generally he doesn't like what I cook as much as what he used to eat in diners and certainly not as much as what he used to make for himself before he met me.

For instance, he used to make a roulade of beef cooked in a Marsala sauce. He would take thin slices of top round or sirloin, dust them with flour, coat one side with crushed dill seeds, roll them around cooked Italian sausage meat, and pierce them with a toothpick. Then he would sauté them in butter and simmer them in a brown Marsala sauce with mushrooms. He would also make roulades of veal stuffed with prosciutto and Gruyère. Another favorite was a meatloaf of veal, pork, and sirloin. It would contain garlic, rosemary, two eggs, and whole-wheat bread crumbs. He would lay smoked bacon underneath it and on top of it.

Now the loaf I make for him is of ground turkey. It, too, has mushrooms, fresh whole-wheat bread crumbs and garlic in it, but in other ways it is not the same. I make it with one egg, celery, leeks, sweet red peppers, salt and pepper, and a dash of nutmeg.

Outdoors on the deck, he eats it and says nothing, gazing over the water past the willow tree. He is calm and contemplative. I don't think he's calm because I'm feeding him so much less meat, but because he is teaching himself to accept what I do. He doesn't like it but knows that I believe I'm doing it for his own good.

When he says nothing about the turkey loaf, I question him, and when I press him to answer, he says that it's all right but he's not excited about it. He excuses himself by saying that in general he's not very excited about food. I disagree, because I have seen him excited about food, though almost never about what I serve him. In fact, I can remember only one occasion on which he was excited by what I served him.

It was the night I made polenta and spicy vegetables for our dinner, though that was not what excited him. The polenta, spreading in a thick ocher circle under the heap of reddish-brown vegetables, looked strange and reminded us both of a cow patty. When he had eaten some of it, though, my husband said it tasted better than it looked, something he has said before about other meals of mine. The cookbook had suggested a certain dessert to follow: a ripe pear, chilled, with walnuts. As we sat down to our meal, I told my husband what I was planning for dessert, though I was not going to bother chilling the pear.

That's one of my problems as a cook—that I don't bother to do each thing the way it should be done. I don't seem to understand the importance of detail, in cooking. My husband does, and when I told him my plan for dessert, he got right up from the table and put the pear in the freezer to chill.

When we came to eat the pear and the walnuts, the

contrast between the cool, juicy sweetness of the fruit and the warmer, oily fragrance of the nuts certainly excited my husband, enough for him to imagine other desserts of fruit—poached figs with ginger, apricot fritters, and sliced blood oranges with pecans. Certainly he was more excited about this dessert than he had been about anything else I had served him. But then he was the one who had put the pear in the freezer, and I've learned by now that when he's involved in preparing a meal, or anything else for that matter, he's more apt to like it.

Henry encounters Jack on the street and asks how his weekend with Laura was. Jack says he hasn't spoken to Laura in at least a month. Henry is angry. He thinks Ellen has been lying to him about Laura. Ellen says she has been telling the truth: Laura told her over the phone that Jack was coming for the weekend to her house up there in the country. Henry is still angry, but now he is angry because he thinks Laura was lying to Ellen when she told her Jack was coming up for the weekend. At this point, with embarrassment, Ellen realizes her mistake: more than one Jack is involved here. Laura said only that Jack was coming to visit her for the weekend, and it was not the Jack that Ellen and Henry know but the Jack that only Ellen knows, and only slightly, who was about to arrive at Laura's house in the country. With some misgiving, she explains this to Henry. Now Henry is even angrier than before, but he is angry because Laura has been seeing a Jack he does not know instead of the Jack he knows. He is angry because the Jack he knows is an old friend of Laura's, whereas the Jack he does not know must be a new lover. Henry declares he will not speak to Laura again except to ask her to send back his keys. He will take her name out of his address book and refuse to hear any further mention of her from Ellen or the Jack he knows. Henry cannot know, since he will not speak to Laura, that in fact a third Jack has become involved in this story, to the distress of the second Jack, for Laura's affections have already strayed from the Jack that Ellen knows only slightly and that Henry does not know, and fastened on a Jack in the country unknown to them all.

Sat down to read Foucault with pencil in hand. Knocked over glass of water onto waiting-room floor. Put down Foucault and pencil, mopped up water, re-filled glass. Sat down to read Foucault with pencil in hand. Stopped to write note in notebook. Took up Foucault with pencil in hand. Counselor beckoned from doorway. Put away Foucault and pencil as well as notebook and pen. Sat with counselor discussing situation fraught with conflict taking form of many heated arguments. Counselor pointed to danger, raised red flag. Left counselor, went to subway. Sat in subway car, took out Foucault and pencil but did not read, thought instead about situation fraught with conflict, red flag, recent argument concerning travel: argument itself became form of travel, each sentence carrying arguers on to next sentence, next sentence on to next, and in the end, arguers were not where they had started, were also tired from traveling and spending so long face-to-face in each other's company. After several stations on subway thinking about argument, stopped thinking and opened Foucault. Found Foucault, in French, hard to understand. Short sentences easier to understand than long ones. Certain long ones under-standable part by part, but so long, forgot beginning before reaching end. Went back to beginning, understood beginning, read on, and again forgot beginning before reaching end. Read on without going back and without understanding, without remembering, and without learning, pencil idle in hand. Came to sentence that was clear, made pencil mark in margin. Mark indicated understanding, indicated forward progress in book. Lifted eyes from Foucault, looked at other passengers. Took out notebook and pen to make note about passengers, made accidental mark with pencil in margin of Foucault, put down notebook, erased mark. Returned thoughts to argument. Argument not only like vehicle, carried arguers forward, but also like plant, grew like hedge, surrounding arguers at first thinly, some light coming through, then more thickly, keeping light out, or darkening light. By argument's end, arguers could not leave hedge, could not leave each other, and light was dim. Thought of question to ask about argument, took out notebook and pen and wrote down. Put away notebook and returned to Foucault. Understood more clearly at which points Foucault harder to understand and at which points easier: harder to understand when sentence was long and noun identifying subject of sentence was left back at beginning, replaced by male or female pronoun, when forgot what noun pronoun replaced and had only pronoun for company traveling through sentence. Sometimes pronoun then giving way in mid-sentence to new noun, new noun in turn replaced by new pronoun which then continued on to end of sentence. Also harder to understand when subject of sentence was noun like thought, absence, law; easier to understand when subject was noun like beach, wave, sand, sanatorium, pension, door, hallway, or civil servant. Before and after sentence about sand, civil servant, or pension, however, came sentence about attraction, neglect, emptiness, absence, or law, so parts of book understood were separated by parts not understood. Put down Foucault and pencil, took out notebook and made note of what was now at least understood about lack of understanding reading Foucault, looked up at other passengers, thought again about argument, made note of same question about argument as before though with stress on different word.

THE MICE

Mice live in our walls but do not trouble our kitchen. We are pleased but cannot understand why they do not come into our kitchen, where we have traps set, as they come into the kitchens of our neighbors. Although we are pleased, we are also upset, because the mice behave as though there were something wrong with our kitchen. What makes this even more puzzling is that our house is much less tidy than the houses of our neighbors. There is more food lying about in our kitchen, more crumbs on the counters and filthy scraps of onion kicked against the base of the cabinets. In fact, there is so much loose food in the kitchen I can only think the mice themselves are defeated by it. In a tidy kitchen, it is a challenge for them to find enough food night after night to survive until spring. They patiently hunt and nibble hour after hour until they are satisfied. In our kitchen, however, they are faced with something so out of proportion to their experience that they cannot deal with it. They might venture out a few steps, but soon the overwhelming sights and smells drive them back into their holes, uncomfortable and embarrassed at not being able to scavenge as they should.

In a town of twelve women there was a thirteenth. No one admitted she lived there, no mail came for her, no one spoke of her, no one asked after her, no one sold bread to her, no one bought anything from her, no one returned her glance, no one knocked on her door; the rain did not fall on her, the sun never shone on her, the day never dawned on her, the night never fell for her; for her the weeks did not pass, the years did not roll by; her house was unnumbered, her garden untended, her path not trod upon, her bed not slept in, her food not eaten, her clothes not worn; and yet in spite of all this she continued to live in the town without resenting what it did to her.

A few years ago, I used to tell myself I wanted to marry a cowboy. Why shouldn't I say this to myself—living alone, excited by the brown landscape, sometimes noticing a cowboy in a pickup truck in my rearview mirror, as I drove on the broad highways of the West Coast? In fact, I realize I would still like to marry a cowboy, though by now I'm living in the East and married already to someone who is not a cowboy.

But what would a cowboy want with a woman like me—an English professor, the daughter of another English professor, not very easygoing? If I have a drink or two, I'm more easygoing, but I still speak correctly and don't know how to joke with people unless I know them well, and often these are university people or the people they live with, who also speak correctly. Although I don't mind them, I feel cut off from all the other people in this country—to mention only this country.

I told myself I liked the way cowboys dressed, starting with the hat, and how comfortable they were in their clothes, so practical, having to do with their work. Many professors seem to dress the way they think a professor should dress, without any real interest or love. Their clothes are too tight or else a few years out of style and just add to the awkwardness of their bodies.

After I was hired to teach for the first time, I bought a briefcase, and then after I started teaching I carried it through the halls like the other professors. I could see that the older professors, mostly men but also some women, were no longer aware of the importance of their briefcases, and that the younger women pretended they weren't aware of it, but the younger men carried their briefcases like trophies.

At that same time, my father began sending me thick envelopes containing material he thought would help me in my classes, including exercises to assign and quotes to use. I didn't read more than a few pages sometimes when I was feeling strong. How could an old professor try to teach a young professor? Didn't he know I wouldn't be able to carry my briefcase through the halls and say hello to my colleagues and students and then go home and read the instructions of the old professor?

In fact, I liked teaching because I liked telling other people what to do. In those days it seemed clearer to me than it does now that if I did something a certain way, it had to be right for other people, too. I was so convinced of it that my students were convinced, too. Still, though I was a teacher outside, I was something else inside. Some of the old professors were also old professors inside, but inside, I wasn't even a young professor. I looked like a woman in glasses, but I had dreams of leading a very different kind of life, the life of a woman who would not wear glasses, the kind of woman I saw from a distance now and then in a bar.

More important than the clothes a cowboy wore, and the way he wore them, was the fact that a cowboy probably wouldn't know much more than he had to. He would think about his work, and about his family, if he had one, and about having a good time, and not much else. I was tired of so much thinking, which was what I did most in those days. I did other things, but I went on thinking while I did them. I might feel something, but I would think about what I was feeling at the same time. I even had to think about what I was thinking and wonder why I was thinking it. When I had the idea of marrying a cowboy I imagined that maybe a cowboy would help me stop thinking so much.

I also imagined, though I was probably wrong about this, too, that a cowboy wouldn't be like anyone I knew—like an old Communist, or a member of a steering committee, a writer of letters to the newspaper, a faculty wife serving tea at a student tea, a professor reading proofs with a sharp pencil and asking everyone to be quiet. I thought that when my mind, always so busy, always going around in circles, always having an idea and then an idea about an idea, reached out to his mind, it would meet something quieter, that there would be more blanks, more open spaces, that some of what he had in his mind might be the sky, clouds, hilltops, and then other concrete things like ropes, saddles, horsehair, the smell of horses and cattle, motor oil, calluses, grease, fences, gullies, dry streambeds, lame cows, stillborn calves, freak calves, veterinarians' visits, treatments, innoculations. I imagined this even though I knew that some of the things I liked that might be in his mind, like the saddles, the saddle sores, the horsehair, and the horses themselves, weren't often a part of the life of a cowboy anymore. As for what I would do in my life with this cowboy, I sometimes imagined myself reading quietly in clean clothes in a nice study, but at other times I imagined myself oiling tack or cooking large quantities of plain food or helping out in the barn in the early morning while the cowboy had both arms inside a cow to turn a calf so it would present properly. Problems and chores like these would be clear and I would be able to handle them in a clear way. I wouldn't stop reading and thinking, but I wouldn't know very many people who did a lot of that, so I would have more privacy in it, because the cowboy, though so close to me all the time, wouldn't try to understand but would leave me alone with it. It would not be an embarrassment anymore.

I thought if I married a cowboy, I wouldn't have to leave the West. I liked the West for its difficulties. First I liked the difficulty of telling when one season was over and another had begun, and then I liked the difficulty of finding any beauty in the landscape where I was. To begin with, I had gotten used to its own kind of ugliness, all those broad highways laid down in the valleys and the new constructions placed up on the bare hillsides. Then I began to find beauty in it, and liked the bareness and the plain brown of the hills in the dry season, and the way the folds in the hills where some dampness tended to linger would fill up with grasses and shrubs and other flowering plants. I liked the plainness of the ocean and the emptiness when I looked out over it. And then, especially since it had been so hard for me to find this beauty, I didn't want to leave it.

I might have gotten the idea of marrying a cowboy from a movie I saw one night in the springtime with a friend of mine who was also a professor—a handsome and intelligent man kinder than I am, but even more awkward around people, forgetting even the names of old friends in his sudden attacks of shyness. He seemed to enjoy the movie, though I have no idea what was going through his mind. Maybe he was imagining a life with the woman in the movie, who was so different from his thin, nervous, and beautiful wife. As we drove away from the movie theater, on one of those broad highways with nothing ahead or behind but taillights and headlights and nothing on either side but darkness, all I wanted to do was go out into the middle of the desert, as far away as possible from everything I had known all my life, and from the university where I was teaching and the towns and the city near it with all the intelligent people who lived and worked in them, writing down their ideas in notebooks and on computers in their offices and their studies at home and taking notes from difficult books. I wanted to leave all this and go out into the middle of the desert and run a motel by myself with a little boy, and have a worn-out cowboy come along, a worn-out middle-aged cowboy, alcoholic if necessary, and marry him. I thought I knew of a little boy I could take with me. Then all I would need would be the aging cowboy and the motel. I would make it a good motel, I would look after it and I would solve any problems sensibly and right away as they came along. I thought I could be a good, tough businesswoman just because I had seen this movie showing this good, tough businesswoman. This woman also had a loving heart and a capacity to understand another fallible human being. The fact is that if an alcoholic cowboy came into my life in any important way I would probably criticize him to death for his drinking until he walked out on me. But at the time I had that strange confidence, born of watching a good movie, that I could be something different from what I was, and I started listening to country Western music on the car radio, though I knew it wasn't written for me.

At that point I met a man in one of my classes who seemed reasonably close to my idea of a cowboy, though now I can't tell exactly why I thought so. He wasn't really like a cowboy, or what I thought a cowboy might be like, so what I wanted must have been something else, and the idea of a cowboy just came up in my mind for the sake of convenience. The facts weren't right. He didn't work as a cowboy but at some kind of job where he glued the bones of chimpanzees together. He played jazz trombone, and on the days when he had a lesson he wore a dark suit to class and carried a black case. He just missed being good-looking, with his square, fleshy, pale face, his dark hair, mustache, dark eyes; just missed being good-looking, not because of his rough cheeks, which were scarred from shrapnel, but because of a loose or wild look about him, his eyes wide open all the time, even when he smiled, and his body very still, only his eyes moving, watching everything, missing nothing. Wary, he was ready to defend himself as though every conversation might also be something of a fight.

One day when a group of us were having a beer together after class, he was quiet, seemed very low, and finally said to us, without raising his eyes, that he thought he might be going to move in with his father and send his little girl back to her mother. He said he didn't think it was fair to keep her because sometimes he would just sit in a chair without speaking—she would try to talk to him and he wouldn't be able to open his mouth, she would keep on trying and he would sit there knowing he had to answer her but unable to.

His rudeness and wildness were comfortable to me at that point, and because he would tease me now and then, I thought he liked me enough so that I could ask him to go out to dinner with me, and finally I did, just to see what would happen. He seemed startled, then pleased to accept, sobered and flattered at this attention from his professor.

The date didn't turn out to be something that would change the direction of my life, though that's not what I was expecting then, only what I thought about afterwards. He was very late coming to pick me up at the graduate-student housing compound where I was staying. Just when I had decided he wasn't coming, after I had spent an hour pacing more and more hopelessly out onto my tiny tree-shaded balcony, which overlooked a playground and the parking lot, and back into my tiny living room, which was crowded with the things of some young couple I didn't know, he came in wearing an old work shirt with the sleeves rolled up and brown corduroys with the cord worn off on the thighs. He stopped and looked around as though he were about to get to work on something, then spotted the piano and bent over it for a moment and played a fast, pretty tune just long enough to make me happy again, then broke it off in the middle.

I was very curious about him, as though everything that added itself to what I knew already would be a revelation. When we got into the car he reached across me and unlocked the glove compartment and when we prepared to get out he reached across me and locked it again. I asked him why he did that, and he lifted up a bundle of papers in the glove compartment and showed me the wooden butt of a gun. He told me a couple of men were after him, and that it had something to do with his little girl.

We parked near the restaurant, he took a gray jacket off a hanger in the car and put it over his arm, and as we walked along he tucked in his shirt and then put on the jacket. I thought to myself this was how a cowboy might do it—carry his gray suit in the car on a hanger, and when he neatened up to go into some place with a woman he would also touch his hair gently.

He drank milk with his Chinese dinner. He talked about his job, offering me pieces of scientific information, and then told some bad jokes. We didn't either of us eat very much, embarrassed, I think, to be alone together like this. He told me that he had married his wife right after he got back from the war. She was half Chinese and half Mexican. He told me his hearing had been damaged in the war and I noticed that he watched my lips as I talked. He told me his balance had been affected, too, and outside the restaurant I noticed how he would veer toward the curb when he walked. He drank milk in the restaurant but beer in the bar where we went to play pool. He put his arm around me outside the bar, but back in the car he said he had to get home to his babysitter. Then he changed his mind and took me to a spot on a cliff that looked out over the ocean and kissed me. Other cars were parked around us, and a pickup truck.

He kissed me a number of times there in his old maroon Ford with the radio on, so that I could have imagined I was a teenager again except that when I was a teenager I had never done anything like that. Then we got out of the car and went to the edge of the cliff to look down at the ocean, the black water of the bay, and the strings of lights that reached out into the water from the town where we had been playing pool. We sat down on the sand not far from the edge of the cliff and he told me a little more about how hard it had been with his wife, how he had tried to get back together with her, how he had done his best to charm her and she wouldn't be charmed. He told me he had been alone with his little girl for six months now, and his wife was coming home in a few days to try living with him again, even though nothing he did had ever worked. He said he wouldn't be able to see me again. I told him I wasn't expecting that anyway, because I was leaving the West soon. It wasn't quite true that I hadn't expected to see him again, but it was true that I was leaving soon. Finally he took me home and kissed me good night.

As far as I could tell, I didn't mind the way the date turned out, though I started crying the next day in my car on my way to the drive-in bank. I thought I was crying for him, his fears, his difficulties, the mysterious men he thought were after him and his daughter, but I was probably crying for myself, out of disappointment, though exactly what I wanted I'm not sure. Months later, after I was living in the East again, I called him long-distance one night after having a couple of beers by myself in my apartment, and when he answered there was noise in the background of people talking and laughing, either his family or a party, I can't remember which, and he sounded just as pleased to hear from me, and flattered, as he had sounded when I asked him out on the date.

I still imagine marrying a cowboy, though less often, and the dream has changed a little. I'm so used to the companionship of my husband by now that if I were to marry a cowboy I would want to take him with me, though he would object strongly to any move in the direction of the West, which he dislikes. So if we went, it would not be as it was in my daydream a few years ago, with me cooking plain food or helping the cowboy with a difficult calf. It would end, or begin, with my husband and me standing awkwardly there in front of the ranch house, waiting while the cowboy prepared our rooms.

When our women had all turned into cedar trees they would group together in a corner of the graveyard and moan in the high wind. At first, with our wives gone, our spirits rose and we all thought the sound was beautiful. But then we ceased to be aware of it, grew uneasy, and quarreled more often among ourselves.

That was during the year of high winds. Never before had such tumult raged in our village. Sparrows could not fly, but swerved and dropped into calm corners; clay tiles tumbled from the roofs and shattered on the pavement. Shrubbery whipped our low windows. Night after night we drank insanely and fell asleep in one another's arms.

When spring came, the winds died down and the sun was bright. At evening, long shadows fell across our floors, and only the glint of a knife blade could survive the darkness. And the darkness fell across our spirits, too. We no longer had a kind word for anyone. We went to our fields grudgingly. Silently we stared at the strangers who came to see our fountain and our church: we leaned against the lip of the fountain, our boots crossed, our maimed dogs shying away from us.

Then the road fell into disrepair. No strangers came. Even the traveling priest no longer dared enter the village, though the sun blazed in the water of the fountain, the valley far below was white with flowering fruit and nut trees, and the heat seeped into the pink stones of the church at noon and ebbed out at dusk. Cats paced silently over the beaten dirt, from doorway to doorway. Birds sang in the woods behind us. We waited in vain for visitors, hunger gnawing at our stomachs.

At last, somewhere deep in the heart of the cedar trees, our wives stirred and thought of us. And lazily, it seemed to us, carelessly, returned home. We looked on their mean lips, their hard eyes, and our hearts melted. We drank in the sound of their harsh voices like men coming out of the desert.

THE CATS IN THE PRISON RECREATION HALL

The problem was the cats in the prison recreation hall. There were feces everywhere. The feces of a cat try to hide in a corner and when discovered look angry and ashamed like a monkey.

The cats stayed in the prison recreation hall when it rained, and since it rained often, the hall smelled bad and the prisoners grumbled. The smell did not come from the feces but from the animals themselves. It was a strong smell, a dizzying smell.

The cats could not be driven away. When shooed, they did not flee out the door but scattered in all directions, running low, their bellies hanging. Many went upward, leaping from beam to beam and resting somewhere high above, so that the prisoners playing ping-pong were aware that although the dome was silent, it was not empty.

The cats could not be driven away because they entered and left the hall through holes that could not be discovered. Their steps were silent; they could wait for a person longer than a person would wait for them.

A person has other concerns, but at each moment in its life, a cat has only one concern. This is what gives it such perfect balance, and this is why the spectacle of a confused or frightened cat upsets us: we feel both pity and the desire to laugh. It faces the source of danger or confusion and its only recourse is to spit a foul breath out between its mottled gums.

The prisoners were all small men that year. They had committed crimes which could not be taken very seriously and they were treated with leniency. Now, although small men are often inclined to take pride in their good health, these prisoners began to develop rashes and eczemas. The backs of their knees and the insides of their elbows stung and their skin flaked all over. They wrote angry letters to the governor of their state, who also happened to be a small man that year. The cats, they said, were causing reactions.

The governor took pity on the prisoners and asked the warden to take care of the problem.

The warden had not been inside the hall in years. He entered it and wandered around, sickened by the curious smell.

In the dead end of a corridor, he cornered an ugly tomcat. The warden was carrying a stick and the cat was armed only with its teeth and claws, besides its angry face. The warden and the cat dodged back and forth for a time, the warden struck out at the cat, and the cat streaked around him and away, making no false moves.

Now the warden saw cats everywhere.

After the evening activities, when the prisoners had been shut up in their cell blocks, the warden returned carrying a rifle. All night long, that night, the prisoners heard the sound of shots coming from the hall. The shots were muffled and seemed to come from a great distance, as though from across the river. The warden was a good shot and killed many cats—cats rained down on him from the dome, cats flipped over and over in the hallways—and yet he still saw shadows flitting by the basement windows as he left the building.

There was a difference now, however. The prisoners' skin condition cleared. Though the bad smell still hung about the building, it was not warm and fresh as it had been. A few cats still lived there, but they had been disoriented by the odors of gunpowder and blood and by the sudden disappearance of their mates and kittens. They stopped breeding and skulked in corners, hissing even when no one was anywhere near them, attacking without provocation any moving thing.

These cats did not eat well and did not clean themselves carefully, and one by one, each in its own way and in its own time died, leaving behind it a different strong smell which hung in the air for a week or two and then dissipated. After some months, there were no cats left in the prison recreation hall. By then, the small prisoners had been succeeded by larger prisoners, and the warden had been replaced by another, more ambitious; only the governor remained in office.

Wife one calls to speak to son. Wife two answers with impatience, gives phone to son of wife one. Son has heard impatience in voice of wife two and tells mother he thought caller was father's sister: raging aunt, constant caller, troublesome woman. Wife one wonders: is she herself perhaps another raging woman, constant caller? No, raging woman but not constant caller. Though, for wife two, also troublesome woman.

After speaking to son, much disturbance in wife one. Wife one misses son, thinks how some years ago she, too, answered phone and talked to husband's raging sister, constant caller, protecting husband from troublesome woman. Now wife two protects husband from troublesome sister, constant caller, and also from wife one, raging woman. Wife one sees this and imagines future wife three protecting husband not only from raging wife one but also from troublesome wife two, as well as constantly calling sister.

After speaking to son, wife one, often raging though now quiet woman, eats dinner alone though in company of large television. Wife one swallows food, swallows pain, swallows food again. Watches intently ad about easy-to-clean stove: mother who is not real mother flips fried egg onto hot burner, then fries second egg and gives cheerful young son who is not real son loving kiss as spaniel who is not real family dog steals second fried egg off plate of son who is not real son. Pain increases in wife one, wife one swallows food, swallows pain, swallows food again, swallows pain again, swallows food again.

THE FISH TANK

I stare at four fish in a tank in the supermarket. They are swimming in parallel formation against a small current created by a jet of water, and they are opening and closing their mouths and staring off into the distance with the one eye, each, that I can see. As I watch them through the glass, thinking how fresh they would be to eat, still alive now, and calculating whether I might buy one to cook for dinner, I also see, as though behind or through them, a larger, shadowy form darkening their tank, what there is of me on the glass, their predator.

A woman has written a story that has a hurricane in
it, and a hurricane usually promises to be interesting.
But in this story the hurricane threatens the city without
actually striking it. The story is flat and even, just as
the earth seems flat and even when a hurricane is
advancing over it, and if she were to show it to a friend,
the friend would probably say that, unlike a hurricane,
this story has no center.

It was not an easy story to write, because it was about
religion, and religion was not something she really
wanted to write about. Something, though, made her
want to write this story. Now that it is finished, it
puzzles her, and there is a peculiar yellow pall over it,
either because of the religion or because of the light
in the sky before the hurricane.

She can't think where the center of the story might
be.

She was reading the Bible in a time of hurricane,
not because she was afraid of a major disaster, though
she was afraid, or because these days also happened to
be the High Holy Days, but because she needed to
know exactly what was in it. She read slowly and took
many notes. Outside her apartment, the weather was
changing: the wind rose, the branches swayed on the

young trees, and the leaves fluttered. She read about Noah and the Ark and tried to picture very exactly what she read, the better to understand it: a man hundreds of years old trying to walk and give directions to his family, the mud covering the earth after the flood receded, the stink of rot, and then the sacrifice of animals and the stink of burning hair, fur, and horn.

She did little else but read the Bible for several days, and she looked out the window often and listened to the news. Certainly the Bible and the hurricane belong in the story, though whether at the center or not she does not know. She had started the story with her landlady. Her landlady, an old woman from Trinidad, was alone in the downstairs hall talking quietly about the Mayor, while she was upstairs, thinking of writing a letter to the President. Her landlady said the red carpet remnant on the hall floor was given to her by her friend the Mayor. She will probably take out the President and the landlady, but leave in the Bible and the hurricane. Perhaps if she takes out things that are not interesting, or do not belong in the story for other reasons, this will give it more of a center, since as soon as there is less in a story, more of it must be in the center.

In another part of the story, a man is very ill and thinks he is dying. He was not dying, he had eaten something that poisoned him and drunk too much on top of it, but he thought he was dying, and telephoned her to come help him. This was at the very moment the hurricane was supposed to strike the city, and some of the windows in the neighborhoods between her house and his were covered with tape in the shape of asterisks. In his room, the blinds were drawn, the light was yellow, and the windows rattled. He lay on his back in bed with a hand on his bare chest. His face was gray.

It is unclear what his place is, in the story. Certainly his illness has little connection with the rest of the story except that it overcame him at the height of the hurricane. But then he also told her something on the phone about blasphemy. He had recently blasphemed in a dreadful way, he said, by committing a certain forbidden act on a Holy Day. What he realized as he did it, he said, was that for complicated reasons he was trying to hurt God, and if he was trying to hurt God he must believe in Him. He had experienced the truth of what he had been taught long ago, that blasphemy proved one's belief in God.

This man, his illness, his fear for his life, and the blasphemy that had caused his illness, as he probably thought, and also something else he said about God that she remembered later, riding a train out of the city, could be at the center of the story, with the Bible and the hurricane at the edge of it, but there may not be enough to tell about him for him to be the center, or this may be the wrong time to tell it.

So there is the hurricane that did not strike the city but cast a yellow light over it, and there is this man, and there is the Bible, but no landlady, no President, and no newscasters, though she watched the news several times a day, every day, to see what the hurricane was going to do. The newscasters would tell her to look out the window and she would look. They would tell her that at that very moment, because the sun had just set, rams' horns were being blown all over the city, and she would be excited, even though she could not hear any rams' horns in her neighborhood. But though the newscasters serve to hold the story together from one day to the next, they are not in themselves very interesting and certainly not central to a story that has trouble finding its center.

In those days she also visited churches and synagogues. The last church she visited was a Baptist congregation in the north of the city. There, large black women in white uniforms asked her to sit down but she was too nervous to sit. Then, standing at the back of the crowded hall, she began to feel faint when a procession of women in red robes came toward her at a stately pace, singing. She left, found the ladies' room, and sat in a stall watching a fly, not sure she would be able to stand up again.

In fact, close to the center of the story may be the moment when she realizes that, even though she is not a believer, she has an unusual, religious sort of peace in her, perhaps because she has been visiting churches and synagogues and studying the Bible, and that this peace has allowed her to accept the possibility of the worst sort of disaster, one even worse than a hurricane.

She rides the train up along the river away from the city. The danger of the hurricane is past. The water in the river has not risen to cover the tracks, though it is close to them. As she looks out at the water, she suddenly remembers the devil. She has not made a place for him in what she might believe, or even in the questions she is asking about what she believes. She has asked several friends whether they thought there was a God, but she has not mentioned the devil to anyone. After she remembers this, she realizes something else: the very fact that she has forgotten the devil must mean he has, at this point, no place in her beliefs, though she thinks she believes in the power of evil.

This comes close to the end of the story as it is now, but she can't really end with the devil and a train ride. So the end is a problem, too, though less of a problem than the center. There may be no center. There may be no center because she is afraid to put any one of these elements in the center—the man, the religion, or the hurricane. Or—which is or is not the same thing—there is a center but the center is empty, either because she has not yet found what belongs there or because it is meant to be empty: there, but empty, in the same way that the man was sick but not dying, the hurricane approached but did not strike, and she had a religious calm but no faith.

L O V E

A woman fell in love with a man who had been dead a number of years. It was not enough for her to brush his coats, wipe his inkwell, finger his ivory comb: she had to build her house over his grave and sit with him night after night in the damp cellar.

We have ideals of being very kind to everyone in the world. But then we are very unkind to our own husband, the person who is closest at hand to us. But then we think he is preventing us from being kind to everyone else in the world. Because he does not want us to know those other people, we think! He would prefer us to stay here in our own house. He says the car is old. We know that really he would prefer us to be acquainted with only a small number of people in the world, as he is. But what he says is that the car would not take us very far. We know he would prefer us to look after our own house and our own family. Our house is not clean, not completely clean. Our family is not completely clean. We think the car would serve us well enough. But he thinks we may want to go out and be kind to other people only because we would prefer not to be at home, because we would prefer not to have to try to be kind only to these three people, of all the people in the world the hardest three for us, though we can easily be kind to so many other people, such as those we meet at the stores, where we go because there our car, he says, may safely take us.

In our home here by the rising sea we will not last much longer. The cold and the damp will certainly get us in the end, because it is no longer possible to leave: the cold has cracked open the only road away from here, the sea has risen and filled the cracks down by the marsh where it is low, has sunk and left salt crystals lining the cracks, has risen again higher and made the road impassable.

The sea washes up through the pipes into our basins, and our drinking water is brackish. Mollusks have appeared in our front yard and our garden and we can't walk without crushing their shells at every step. At every high tide the sea covers our land, leaving pools, when it ebbs, among our rosebushes and in the furrows of our rye field. Our seeds have been washed away; the crows have eaten what few were left.

Now we have moved into the upper rooms of the house and stand at the window watching the fish flash through the branches of our peach tree. An eel looks out from below our wheelbarrow.

What we wash and hang out the upstairs window to dry freezes: our shirts and pants make strange writhing shapes on the line. What we wear is always damp now, and the salt rubs against our skin until we are red and sore. Much of the day, now, we stay in bed under heavy, sour blankets; the wooden walls are wet through; the sea enters the cracks at the windowsills and trickles down to the floor. Three of us have died of pneumonia and bronchitis at different hours of the morning before daybreak. There are three left, and we are all weak, can't sleep but lightly, can't think but with confusion, don't speak, and hardly see light and dark anymore, only dimness and shadow.

ODD BEHAVIOR

You see how circumstances are to blame. I am not really an odd person if I put more and more small pieces of shredded Kleenex in my ears and tie a scarf around my head: when I lived alone I had all the silence I needed.

We were caretakers for most of that year, from early
fall until summer. There was a house and grounds to
look after, two dogs, and two cats. We fed the cats,
one white and one calico, who lived outside and ate
their meals on the kitchen windowsill, sparring in the
sunlight as they waited for their food, but we did not
keep the house very clean, or the weeds cut in the
yard, and our employers, kind people though they
were, probably never quite forgave us for what happened to one of the dogs.

We hardly knew what a clean house should look
like. We would begin to think we were quite tidy, and
then we would see the dust and clutter of the rooms,
and the two hearths covered with ash. Sometimes we
argued about it, sometimes we cleaned it. The oil stove
became badly blocked and we did nothing for days
because the telephone was out of order. When we
needed help, we went to see the former caretakers, an
old couple who lived with their cages of breeding can-
aries in the nearest village. The old man came by
sometimes, and when he saw how the grass had grown
so tall around the house, he scythed it without comment.

What our employers needed most from us was simply that we stay in the house. We were not supposed to leave it for more than a few hours, because it had been robbed so often. We left it overnight only once, to celebrate New Year's Eve with a friend many miles away. We took the dogs with us on a mattress in the back of the car. We stopped at village fountains along the way and sprinkled water on their backs. We had too little money, anyway, to go anywhere. Our employers sent us a small amount each month, most of which we spent immediately on postage, cigarettes, and groceries. We brought home whole mackerels, which we cleaned, and whole chickens, which we beheaded and cleaned and prepared to roast, tying their legs together. The kitchen often smelled of garlic. We were told many times that year that garlic would give us strength. Sometimes we wrote letters home asking for money, and sometimes a check was sent for a small sum, but the bank took weeks to cash it.

We could not go much farther than the closest town to shop for food and to a village half an hour away over a small mountain covered with scrub oaks. There we left our sheets, towels, table linen, and other laundry to be washed, as our employers had instructed us to do, and when we picked it up a week later, we sometimes stayed to see a movie. Our mail was delivered to the house by a woman on a motorcycle.

But even if we had had the money, we would not have gone far, since we had chosen to live there in that house, in that isolation, in order to do work of our own, and we often sat inside the house trying to work, not always succeeding. We spent a great deal of time sitting inside one room or another looking down at our work and then up and out the window, though there was not much to see, one bit of landscape or another depending on which room we were in—trees, fields, clouds in the sky, a distant road, distant cars on the road, a village that lay on the horizon to the west of us, piled around its square church tower like a mirage, another village on a hilltop to the north of us across the valley, a person walking or working in a field, a bird or a pair of birds walking or flying, the ruined outbuilding not far from the house.

The dogs stayed near us almost all the time, sleeping in tight curls. If we spoke to them, they looked up with the worried eyes of old people. They were pure-bred yellow Labradors, brother and sister. The male was large, muscular, perfectly formed, of a blond color so light he was nearly white, with a fine head and a lovely broad face. His nature was simple and good. He ran, sniffed, came when we called, ate, and slept. Strong, adept, and willing, he retrieved as long as we asked him to, running down a cliff of sand no matter how steep or how long, plunging into a body of water in pursuit of a stick. Only in villages and towns did he turn shy and fearful, trembling and diving toward the shelter of a café table or a car.

His sister was very different, and as we admired her
brother for his simple goodness and beauty, we admired
her for her peculiar sense of humor, her reluctance,
her cunning, her bad moods, her deviousness. She was
calm in villages and cities and would not retrieve at
all. She was small, with a rusty-brown coat, and not
well formed, a barrel of a body on thin legs and a face
like a weasel.

Because of the dogs, we went outside the house often
in the course of the day. Sometimes one of us would
have to leave the warm bed at five in the morning and
hurry down the cold stone steps to let them out, and
they were so eager that they leaked and left a pattern
of drops on the red tiles of the kitchen and the patio.
As we waited for them, we would look up at the stars,
bright and distinct, the whole sky having shifted from
where it was when we last saw it.

In the early fall, as grape-pickers came into the
neighboring fields to harvest, snails crept up the outside
of the windowpanes, their undersides greenish-gold.
Flies infested the rooms. We swatted them in the wide
bands of sunlight that came through the glass doors of
the music room. They tormented us while alive, then
died in piles on the windowsills, covering our notebooks and papers. They were one of our seven plagues,
the others being the fighter jets that thundered suddenly
over our roof, the army helicopters that batted their
more leisurely way over the treetops, the hunters who

roamed close to the house, the thunderstorms, the two thieving cats, and, after a time, the cold.

The guns of the hunters boomed from beyond the hills or under our windows, waking us early in the morning. Men walked alone or in pairs, sometimes a woman trailed by a small child, spaniels loping out of sight and smoke rising from the mouths of the rifles. When we were in the woods, we would find a hunter's mess by the ruins of a stone house where he had settled for lunch—a plastic wine bottle, a glass wine bottle, scraps of paper, a crumpled paper bag, and an empty cartridge box. Or we would come upon a hunter squatting so motionless in the bushes, his gun resting in his arms, that we did not see him until we were on top of him, and even then he did not move, his eyes fixed on us.

In the village café, at the end of the day, the owner's young son, in olive-green pants, would slip around the counter and up the stairs with his two aged, slinking, tangerine-colored dogs, at the same time that women would come in with the mushrooms they had gathered just before dusk. Cartridge cases peppered the ground across a flat field near the house, one of the odd waste patches that lay in this valley of cultivated fields. Its dry autumn grass was strewn with boulders, among them two abandoned cars. Here from one direction came the smell of wild thyme, from the other the smell of sewage from a sewage bed.

We visited almost no one, only a farmer, a butcher, and a rather pompous retired businessman from the city. The farmer lived alone with his dog and his two cats in a large stone house a field or two away. The businessman, whose hyphenated name in fact contained the word "pomp," lived in a new house in the closest village, to the west of us across the fields. The young butcher lived with his childless wife in town, and we would sometimes encounter him there moving meat across the street from his van to his shop. Cradling a beef carcass or a lamb in his arms, he would stop to talk to us in the sunlight, a wary smile on his face. When he was finished working for the day, he often went out to take photographs. He had studied photography through a correspondence course and received a degree. He photographed town festivals and processions, fairs and shooting matches. Sometimes he took us with him. Now and then a stranger came to the house by mistake. Once it was a young girl who entered the kitchen suddenly in a gust of wind, pale, thin, and strange, like a stray thought.

Because we had so little money, our amusements were simple. We would go out into the sun that beat down on the white gravel and shone off the leaves of the olive tree and toss pebbles one by one, overhand, from a distance of ten feet or so into a large clay urn that stood among the rosemary plants. We did this as a contest with each other, but also alone when we were

finished working or couldn't work. One would be working and hear the dull click, over and over, of a pebble
striking the urn and falling back onto the gravel, and
the more resonant pock of the pebble landing inside
the urn, and would know the other was outside.

When the weather grew too cold, we stayed inside
and played gin rummy. By the middle of winter, when
only a few rooms in the house were heated, we were
playing so much, day and night, that we organized our
games into tournaments. Then, for a few weeks, we
stopped playing and studied German in the evenings
by the fire. In the spring, we went back to our pebble
game.

Nearly every afternoon, we took the dogs for a walk.
On the coldest days of winter, we went out only long
enough to gather kindling wood and pine cones for the
fire. On warmer days, we went out for an hour or more
at a time, most often into the government forest that
spread for miles on a plateau above and behind the
house, sometimes into the fields of vines or lavender
in the valley, or into the meadows, or across to the far
side of the valley, into old groves of olive trees. We
were surrounded for so long by scrub brush, rocks,
pine trees, oaks, red earth, fields, that we felt enclosed
by them even once we were back inside the house.

We would walk, and return with burrs in our socks
and scratches on our legs and arms where we had
pushed through the brambles to get up into the forest,

and go out again the next day and walk, and the dogs always trusted that we were setting out in a certain direction for a reason, and then returning home for a reason, but in the forest, which seemed so endless, there was hardly a distinguishing feature that could be taken as a destination for a walk, and we were simply walking, watching the sameness pass on both sides, the thorny, scrubby oaks growing densely together along the dusty track that ran quite straight until it came to a gentle bend and perhaps a slight rise and then ran straight again.

If we came home by an unfamiliar route, skirting the forest, avoiding a deeply furrowed, overgrown field and then stepping into the edge of a reedy marsh, veering close to a farmyard, where a farmer in blue and his wife in red were doing chores trailed by their dog, we felt so changed ourselves that we were surprised nothing about home had changed: for a moment the placidity of the house and yard nearly persuaded us we had not even left.

Between the forest and the fields, in the thickets of underbrush, we would sometimes come upon a farmhouse in ruins, with a curving flight of deep stone steps, worn at the edges, leading to an upper story that was now empty air, brambles and nettles and mint growing up inside and around it, and sometimes, nearby, an ancient, awkward and shaggy fruit tree, half its branches dead. In the form of this farmhouse, we recognized our own house. We went up the same curving flight of stone steps to bed at night. The animals had lived downstairs in our house, too—our vaulted dining room had once been a sheepfold.

Sometimes, in our walks, we came upon inexplicable things, once, in the cinders of an abandoned fire, two dead jackrabbits. Sometimes we lost our way, and were still lost after the sun had set, when we would start to run, and run without tiring, afraid of the dark, until we saw where we were again.

We had visitors who came from far away to stay with us for several days and sometimes several weeks, sometimes welcome, sometimes less so, as they stayed on and on. One was a young photographer who had worked with our employer and was in the habit of stopping at the house. He would travel through the region on assignments for his magazine, always taking his pictures at dawn or at sunset when the shadows were long. For every night he stayed with us, he paid us the amount he would have paid for a room at a good hotel, since he traveled on a company expense account. He was a small, neat man with a quick, toothy smile. He came alone, or he came with his girlfriend.

He played with the dogs, fondling them, wrestling with them overhead as we sat in the room below trying to work, while we spoke against him angrily, to ourselves. Or he and his girlfriend ironed their clothes above us, with noises we did not at first understand, the stiff cord knocking and sliding against the floorboards. It was hard enough for us to work, sometimes.

They were curiously disorganized, and when they went out on an errand left water coming to a boil on the stove or the sink full of warm soapy water as though they were still at home. Or when they returned from an errand, they left the doors wide open so that the cold air and the cats came in. They were still at breakfast close to noon, and left crumbs on the table. Late in the evening, sometimes, we would find the girlfriend asleep on the sofa.

But we were lonely, and the photographer and his girlfriend were friendly, and they would sometimes cook dinner for us, or take us out to a restaurant. A visit from them meant money in our pockets again.

At the beginning of December, when we began to have the oil stove going full blast in the kitchen all day, the dogs slept next to it while we worked at the dining-room table. We watched through the window as two men returned to work in a cultivated field, one on a tractor and one behind a plow that had been sitting for weeks growing rusty, after opening perhaps ten furrows. Violent high winds sometimes rose during the night and then continued blowing all day so that the birds had trouble flying and dust sifted down through the floorboards. Sometimes one of us would get up in the night, hearing a shutter bang, and go out in pajamas onto the tiles of the garage roof to tie it back again or remove it from its hinge.

A rainstorm would last hours, soaking the ruined outbuilding nearby, darkening its stones. The air in the morning would be soft and limp. After the constant dripping of the rain or wuthering of the wind, there was sometimes complete silence, minute after minute, and then abruptly the rocky echoes of a plane far away in the sky. The light on the wet gravel outside the house was so white, after a storm, it looked like snow.

By the middle of the month, the trees and bushes had begun to lose their leaves and in a nearby field a stone shed, its black doorway overgrown by brambles, gradually came into view.

A flock of sheep gathered around the ruined outbuilding, fat, long-tailed, a dirty brown color, with pale scrawny lambs. Jostling one another, they poured up out of the ruin, climbing the tumble-down walls, the little ones crying in high human voices over the dull clamor of the bells. The shepherd, dressed all in brown with a cap pulled low over his eyes, sat eating on the grass by the woodpile, his face glowing and his chin unshaven. When the sheep became too active, he grunted and his small black dog raced once around the side of the flock and the sheep cantered away in a forest of stick-like legs. When they came near again, streaming out between the walls, the dog sent them flying again. When they disappeared into the next field, the shepherd continued to sit for a while, then moved off slowly, in his baggy brown pants, a leather pouch hanging on long straps down his back, a light stick in one hand, his coat flung over his shoulder, the little black dog charging and veering when he whistled.

One afternoon we had almost no money left, and almost no food. Our spirits were low. Hoping to be invited to dinner, we dropped in on the businessman and his wife. They had been upstairs reading, and came down one after the other holding their reading glasses in their hands, looking tired and old. We saw that when they were not expecting company, they had in their living room a blanket and a sleeping bag arranged over the two armchairs in front of the television. They invited us to have dinner with them the next night.

When we went to their house the next night, we were offered rum cocktails by Monsieur Assiez-de-Pompignan before dinner and afterward we watched a movie with them. When it ended, we left, hurrying to our car against the wind, through the narrow, shuttered streets, dust flying in our teeth.

The following day, for dinner, we had one sausage. The only money left now was a pile of coins on the living-room table collected from saucers around the house and amounting to 2.97 francs, less than fifty cents, but enough to buy something for dinner the next day.

Then we had no money at all anywhere in the house, and almost nothing left to eat. What we found, when we searched the kitchen carefully, was some onions, an old but unopened box of pastry crust mix, a little fat, and a little dried milk. Out of this, we realized, we could make an onion pie. We made it, baked it, cut ourselves two pieces, and put the rest back in the hot oven to cook a little more while we ate. It was surprisingly good. Our spirits lifting, we talked as we ate and forgot all about the pie as it went on baking. By the time we smelled it, it had burned too badly to be saved.

In the afternoon of that day, we went out onto the gravel, not knowing what to do now. We tossed pebbles for a while, there in the boiling sun and the cool air, saying very little because we had no answer to our problem. Then we heard the sound of an approaching car. Along the bumpy dirt road that led to our house from the main road, past the house of the weekend people, of pink stucco with black ironwork, and then past a vineyard on one side and a field on the other, came the photographer in his neat rented car. By pure chance, or like an angel, he was arriving to rescue us at the very moment we had used up our last resource.

We were not embarrassed to say we had no money, and no food either, and he was pleased to invite us out to dinner. He took us into town to a very good restaurant on the main square where the rows of plantain trees stood. A television crew were also dining there, twelve at the table, including a hunchback. By the large, bright fire on one wall, three old women sat knitting: one with liver spots covering her face and hands, the second pinched and bony, the third younger and merrier but slow-witted. The photographer fed us well on his expense account. He stayed with us that night and a few nights after, leaving us with several fifty-franc notes, so we were all right for a while, since a bottle of local wine, for instance, cost no more than one franc fifty.

When winter set in, we closed one by one the other rooms in the house and confined ourselves to the kitchen with its fat oil-burning stove, the vaulted dining room with its massive oak table where we played cards in the thick heat from the kitchen, the music room with its expensive electric heater burning our legs, and at the top of the stone stairway the unheated bedroom with its floor of red tiles so vast there was ample time for it to dip down in the center and rise again on its way to the single small casement window that looked out onto the almond tree and the olive tree below. The house had a different feeling to it when the wind was blowing and parts of it were darkened because we had closed the shutters.

Larks fluttered over the fields in the afternoons, showing silver. The long, straight, deeply rutted road to the village turned to soft mud. In certain lights, the inner walls of the ruined outbuilding were as rosy as a seashell. The dogs sighed heavily as they lay down on the cold tiles, closing their almond-shaped eyes. When they were let out into the sunlight, they fought, panting and scattering gravel. The shadow of the almond tree in the bright, hard sunlight flowed over the gravel like a dark river and lapped up against the wall of the house.

One night, during a heavy rainstorm, we went to the farmer's house for dinner. Nothing grew around his house, not even grass; there was only the massive stone house in a yard of deep mud. The front door was heavy to push open. The entryway was filled with a damp, musty smell from the truffles hanging in a leather pouch from a peg. Sacks full of seed and grain lined the wall.

With the farmer, we went out to the side of the house to collect eggs for dinner. Under the house, in the pens where he had once kept sheep, hens roosted now, their faces sharp in the beam of his flashlight. He gathered the eggs, holding the flashlight in one hand, and gave them to us to carry. The umbrella, as we started back around to the front of the house, turned inside out in the wind.

The kitchen was warm from the heat of a large oil stove. The oven door was open and a cat sat inside looking out. When he was in the house, the farmer spent most of his time in the kitchen. When he had something to throw away, he threw it out the window, burying it later. The table was crowded with bottles—vinegar, oil, his own wine in whiskey bottles which he had brought up from the cellar—and among them cloth napkins and large lumps of sea salt. Behind the table was a couch piled with coats. Two rifles hung in racks against the wall. Taped to the refrigerator was a photograph of the farmer and the truck he used to drive from Paris to Marseille.

For dinner he gave us leeks with oil and vinegar, bits of hard sausage and bread, black olives like cardboard, and scrambled eggs with truffles. He dried lettuce leaves by shaking them in a dishtowel and gave us a salad full of garlic, and then some Roquefort. He told us that his first breakfast, before he went out to work in the fields, was a piece of bread and garlic. He called himself a Communist and talked about the Resistance, telling us that the people of the area knew just who the collaborators were. The collaborators stayed at home out of sight, did not go to the cafés much, and in fact would be killed immediately if there was trouble, though he did not say what he meant by trouble. He had opinions about many things, even the Koran, in which, he said, lying and stealing were not considered sins, and he had questions for us: he wondered if it was the same year over there, in our country.

To get to his new, clean bathroom, we took the flashlight and lit our way past the head of the stairs

and through an empty, high-ceilinged room of which
we could see nothing but a great stone fireplace. After
dinner, we listened in silence to a record of revolu-
tionary songs which he took from a pile on the floor,
while he grew sleepy, yawning and twiddling his
thumbs.

When we returned home, we let the dogs out, as
we always did, to run around before they were shut in
for the night. The hunting season had begun again.
We should not have let the dogs out loose, but we did
not know that. More than an hour passed and the
female came back but her brother did not. We were
afraid right away, because he never stayed out more
than an hour or so. We called and called, near the
house, and then the next morning, when he had still
not returned, we walked through the woods in all directions, calling and searching among the trees.

We knew he would not have stayed away so long
unless he had somehow been stopped from coming
back. He could have wandered into the nearest village,
lured by the scent of a female in heat. He could have
been spotted near the road and taken by a passing
motorist. He could have been stolen by a hunter, someone avid for a good-natured, handsome hunting dog,
proud to show it off in a smoke-filled café. But we
believed first, and longest, that he lay in the underbrush
poisoned, or caught in a trap, or wounded by a bullet.

Day after day passed and he did not come home and we had no news of him. We drove from village to village asking questions, and put up notices with his photograph attached, but we also knew that the people we talked to might lie to us, and that such a beautiful dog would probably not be returned.

People called us who had a yellow dog, or had found a stray, but each time we went to see it, it was not much like our dog. Because we did not know what had happened to him, because it was always possible that he might return, it was hard for us to accept the fact that he was gone. That he was not our dog only made it worse.

After a month, we still hoped the dog would return, though signs of spring began to appear and other things came along to distract us. The almond tree blossomed with flowers so white that against the soft plowed field beyond them they were almost blue. A pair of magpies came to the scrub oak beside the woodpile, fluttering, squawking, diving obliquely down.

The weekend people returned, and every Sunday they called out to each other as they worked the long strip of earth in the field below us. The dog went to the border of our land and barked at them, tense on her stiff legs.

Once we stopped to talk to a woman at the edge of the village and she showed us her hand covered with dirt from digging in the ground. Behind her we could see a man leading another man back into his garden to give him some herbs.

Drifts of daffodils and narcissus bloomed in the fields. We gathered a vase full of them and slept with them in the room, waking up drugged and sluggish. Irises bloomed and then the first roses opened, yellow. The flies became numerous again, and noisy.

We took long walks again, with one dog now. There were bugs in the wiry, stiff grass near the house, small cracks in the dirt, ants. In the field, purple clover grew around our ankles, and large white and yellow daisies at our knees. Blood-red bumblebees landed on buttercups as high as our hands. The long, lush grass in the field rose and fell in waves before the wind, and near us in a thick grove of trees dead branches clacked together. Whenever the wind died, we could hear the trickle of a swollen stream as though it were falling into a stone basin.

In May, we heard the first nightingale. Just as the night fully darkened, it began to sing. Its song was not really unlike the song of a mockingbird, with warbles, and twitters, and trills, warbles, chirps, and warbles again, but it issued in the midst of the silence of the night, in the dark, or in the moonlight, from a spot mysteriously hidden among the black branches.

AGREEMENT

First she walked out, and then while she was out he walked out. No, before she walked out, he walked out on her, not long after he came home, because of something she said. He did not say how long he would be gone or where he was going, because he was angry. He did not say anything except "That's it." Then, while he was out, she walked out on him and went down the road with the children. Then, while she was out, he came back, and when she did not return and it grew dark, he went out looking for her. She returned without seeing him, and after she had been back some time, she walked out again with the children to find him. Later, he said she had walked out on him, and she agreed that she had walked out on him, but said she had only walked out on him after he walked out on her. Then he agreed that he had walked out on her, but only after she said something she should not have said. He said she should agree that she should not have said what she said and that she had caused the evening's harm. She agreed that she should not have said what she said, but then went on to say that the trouble between them had started before, and if she agreed she had caused the evening's harm, he should agree he had caused what started the trouble before. But he would not agree to that, not yet anyway.

A man has been making deliveries in the garment district for years now: every morning he takes the same garments on a moving rack through the streets to a shop and every evening takes them back again to the warehouse. This happens because there is a dispute between the shop and the warehouse which cannot be settled: the shop denies it ever ordered the clothes, which are badly made and of cheap material and by now years out of style; while the warehouse will not take responsibility because the clothes cannot be returned to the wholesalers, who have no use for them. To the man all this is nothing. They are not his clothes, he is paid for this work, and he intends to leave the company soon, though the right moment has not yet come.

DISAGREEMENT

He said she was disagreeing with him. She said no, that was not true, he was disagreeing with her. This was about the screen door. That it should not be left open was her idea, because of the flies; his was that it could be left open first thing in the morning, when there were no flies on the deck. Anyway, he said, most of the flies came from other parts of the building: in fact, he was probably letting more of them out than in.

In our town there is an actor, H.—a tall, bold, feverish sort of man—who easily fills the theater when he plays Othello, and about whom the women here become very excited. He is handsome enough compared to the other men, though his nose is somewhat thick and his torso rather short for his height. His acting is stiff and inflexible, his gestures obviously memorized and mechanical, and yet his voice is strong enough to make one forget all that. On the nights when he is unable to leave his bed because of illness or intoxication— and this happens more often than one would imagine—the part is taken by J., his understudy. Now, J. is pale and small, completely unsuitable for the part of a Moor; his legs tremble as he comes onstage and faces the many empty seats. His voice hardly carries beyond the first few rows, and his small hands flutter uselessly in the smoky air. We feel only pity and irritation as we watch him, and yet by the end of the play we find ourselves unaccountably moved, as though something timid and sad in Othello's character had been conveyed to us in spite of ourselves. But the mannerisms and skill of H. and J.—which we analyze minutely when we visit together in the afternoons and contemplate even when we are alone, after dinner—

suddenly seem insignificant when the great Sparr
comes down from the city and gives us a real performance of Othello. Then we are so carried away, so
exhausted with emotion, that it is impossible to speak
of what we feel. We are almost grateful when he is
gone and we are left with H. and J., imperfect as they
are, for they are familiar to us and comfortable, like
our own people.

WHAT WAS INTERESTING

It is hard for her to write this story, too, or rather she
should say it is hard for her to write it well. She has
shown it to a friend, and he has said it needs to be
more interesting. She is disappointed, even though she
knew that only one part of it was interesting. She tries
to think why the rest is not.

Maybe there is no way to make it interesting, because
it is so simple: a woman, slightly drunk but not too
drunk to discuss a plan for the summer, was put into
a cab and told to go home by her lover, the man with
whom she thought she was going to discuss this plan.

She asks her friend if this, at least, was something
that would hurt a woman, or if this was nothing. He
thinks it would hurt, and she is right about that much,
but it is not very interesting.

He had put her into a cab with two men who were
not pleased to be riding with her, as she was not pleased
to be riding with them, because of some complicated
events that had occurred years before. She was talking
politely to them but feeling angry at the man who had
done this to her.

It is not entirely clear, in the story, why being put
in a cab by this man should cause so much anger in
her. Or rather, it is perfectly clear to her, but hard to

[70]

explain to anyone else, though she knows that anyone else, put in the same cab with the same two men, would be angry.

As soon as she arrived home she telephoned him. She raged at him and he laughed, she raged more and he gave her a slight apology and laughed more and said he was sleepy and wanted to go to bed. She hung up. She went on crying and then began drinking. She was so angry she would have been happy to take her fists to him, but he was not there, he was sleeping and probably smiling in his sleep. As she drank she thought hard, and angrily.

What was he trying to do to her this time? she wondered. She and he did not have many chances to be together, and there they were sitting across from each other at dinner, and they had recently started talking about a plan to go away together in the summer, which they had never done before, or even talked about doing before, and he had even sent her a photograph of the house. They had said that after dinner they would talk about it more, and she was very happy about all this, and felt that at last their love was becoming something solid, something she could count on. And then, when she was prepared to walk off with him down the street, her head pleasantly light, her stomach comfortably full, he had suddenly, without warning, taken her arm and led her up to a taxi just as these two men were getting into it, and because there were other people there they both knew, she couldn't say anything but had to pretend this was something she did not mind. And what did he mean by it? What was she supposed to think now, and what was she supposed to do?

At a certain point in her angry thinking she decided she had to give up the idea of a summer plan with him. If he had done this now, what would he do to her during the summer, and, even worse, when the summer was over? And now she drank more to give vent to her disappointment.

The fact that they were involved in a love affair ought to have been interesting, because any kind of affair is usually more interesting than no affair, as two people in a story should be more interesting than one, and a difficult love affair should be more interesting than an easy one. As, for example, a happy woman walking arm in arm with her lover after a noisy restaurant dinner with friends, enjoying the fact that he is so tall and the feel of his smooth hair under her palm when she reaches up, walking with him and discussing summer plans, as she had been sure they were going to do, may be less interesting than being put into a cab with embarrassing haste and awkwardness, or finding a pair of keys that have been lost, as she did later, and then certainly the idea of a key is more interesting than the idea of a cab, and the idea of something lost and then found is more interesting than the idea of already knowing where she was, that is, in the cab and then at home, though it was true that in a more general way she certainly did not know where she was with him, what he expected from her and what he expected would happen to them.

The love affair as they conducted it was irregular, intermittent, and painful to her, painful because in the arrangements they made at long intervals, after months had gone by, he always did something she had not known he was going to do and it was often in contradiction to a plan they had made. She would borrow an apartment especially so that they could have a comfortable place to meet, and he would agree to come there late in the evening, and then he would not come, and after calling him where he was, and hearing his sleepy voice, she would pace from room to room in the borrowed apartment wringing her hands. On another occasion he would say firmly that he would not be coming to the borrowed apartment, and then come to her there without warning. Or they would meet for lunch and nothing more, and then he would suddenly propose that they go to a motel. In the motel, to her surprise, he would say he wanted to keep the room and meet there that night, and she would be happy, and all evening, at home, would wait for him to call and say when he could meet her, and then finally she would call him and hear him say he had not kept the room and could not see her.

But if he always did what she did not expect him to do, and if she knew this, why didn't she think ahead and see that whatever he said he was going to do, he would not do? Though she was not a stupid woman, she did not do this. And what he did that was unexpected was also unkind, almost every time, but perhaps that was more interesting than if he had been kind and reliable, as she wanted him to be, as well as charming and open to her, as he often was: how happy he had looked the last time she had seen him, sitting by her in a bar where they had just met, purely happy in his face, until she said he looked happy and asked why, and he said a few other things and then the truth, that he was happy to see her, after which he looked just slightly less happy.

She was not yet quite finished with crying and raging, but unable to stay there in her apartment, in a place that seemed to contain only her and what had happened and the disappointment of it. She was on her knees on her living-room rug, trying to think where she had put some keys, the keys to a friend's apartment. She wanted to go to this apartment even though she knew the friend was not home and would not be coming home. She could not have gone to him with her trouble, and she supposed, even through the fog of her drunkenness, that she should not go to his apartment with her trouble either. But she would not be stopped from something she wanted so badly. She needed to let the walls of a different place that belonged to a different time relieve her, a little, of herself and what had just happened.

She took a large, heavy drawer out of her bureau and emptied it on the rug. It was awkward to carry and awkward to turn over. She went through everything in it, not seeing very well, but couldn't find the keys, and put everything back, and put the drawer back in the bureau. Then she took a shoe box down from a shelf, lighter and easier to carry. She emptied it on the rug, but the keys weren't there either, so she was still on her knees, crying, and then lying face down on the rug, because she couldn't find the keys. If she couldn't find them, she didn't know what she would do with herself.

She stopped crying, washed and dried her face, and tried to remember where she had last seen them. Then she remembered that they weren't loose, but sealed in a white envelope, and once she remembered that, she knew where she had seen that crumpled envelope recently, and found it in a wooden tray on her desk. She put the keys in her pocket, called a taxi, left the apartment, rode through the silent streets of several different neighborhoods, past two darkened hospitals, to her friend's apartment, and once inside fell asleep on his living-room rug, a thicker and more comfortable rug than her own.

She woke up when the clean light of dawn was coming through his tall windows, and left the apartment soon after, to avoid meeting him. By now she could return to her own apartment, as though she had climbed up to some high, difficult place during the night and climbed down again by morning.

She would never tell her friend she had slept in his apartment. It had been a long time since she had used his keys. His reaction, if he knew, would be interesting. In fact, this friend would possibly have been the most interesting person in the story, if she had put him instead of his apartment into it.

She was sick that day from all she had drunk. It would be more interesting to be well after drinking so much than to be sick, but she preferred being sick to being well that day, as though it were a celebration of the change that had happened, that she would not be sitting out in the Mediterranean sunshine with her lover that summer. After this, she would have almost nothing more to do with him. She would not answer his letters, and would barely speak to him if she chanced to meet him, but this anger of hers, lasting so long, was certainly more interesting to her, because in the end she found it harder to explain, than the fact that she had loved him so long.

Today I am riding in a canopied car on rubber wheels through Jungle Larry's African Safari. We pass a strangler fig tree and some caged cougars. A female leopard hides from us behind a rock. High up on the trunk of a palm in the Orchid Cathedral, one flower blooms beside a rusty faucet. Afterward we throw our trash into the mouth of a yawning plaster lion and leave for the Seminole Indian Village.

The Village is closed, and though the Village Shop is open we do not buy anything, perhaps because the Indians that wait on us and watch us pick through the beaded goods are so very sullen.

Later I sit in a short row of people at the front of an air boat, and with an unpleasant racket we skim the saw grass, moving fast suddenly. Animals everywhere in the mangrove swamp are disturbed, and one by one, with difficulty, herons and egrets rise up before us for miles around into the white sky.

All day I have been looking at a landscape charged with the sun, and when as instructed by the captain of the air boat I watched the water for alligators, the broken light of the reflected sun sparkled painfully. Now it is evening and my eyes ache as I sit in the lamplight incapable of thinking.

I look at what is around me: the papered walls, the gold-leafed decorations, the table in lamplight, my hands on the table, and in particular the back of my right hand on which today a woman has stamped the figure of a huddled monkey that is now becoming indistinct and ugly, and though I try again and again I can't remember exactly where or why this happened.

THE FAMILY

In the playground near the river, toward evening, in the lowering sun, on the green grass, only one family. Swings creak and cry out going back and forth. Shadows of swinging children foreshorten, fly over the grass into the weeds. (1) Fat young white woman pulls white baby by one arm onto quilt spread on grass. (2) Little black boy struggles with older black girl over swing, (3) is ordered to sit down on grass, (4) stands sullen while (5) fat white woman heaves to her feet, walks to him, and smacks him. (6) Little black boy whimpers, lies on his back on grass while (7) fat white woman plays with baby and (8) young black man orders black girl off swing. (9) Young black man begins wrestling in play with long-haired white girl who (10) protests while (11) tall, bony, wrinkled, mustachioed white man in baseball cap stands with arms crossed, back hunched, walkie-talkie attached to right hip and (12) black girl lies down with face in baby's face. (13) Baby peers up and around black girl when (14) white girl protests more loudly as (15) young black man slaps her buttocks and (16) older white man watches with arms crossed. (17) White girl breaks free of young black man and runs toward river crying as (18) young black man runs easily after her and

(19) older white man in baseball cap runs awkwardly after her, one hand on walkie-talkie at his hip. (20) Young black man picks up white girl and carries her back to fat young white woman who (21) takes her onto her lap as (22) little black boy sits up in grass and watches. (23) White girl squirms in arms of young white woman, breaks free and runs again, crying, toward river. (24) Black girl, taller, follows, overtakes her, lifts and carries her back. (25) Young white woman holds white girl who struggles, hair covering her face, while (26) black girl swings on swing holding white baby and (27) white man stands still, back hunched, hips forward, eyes invisible under visor of baseball cap. (28) Young black man goes off toward concrete hut in setting sun and (29) returns to call out to white woman, who (30) leaves white girl and follows after him with baby to concrete hut while (31) black girl continues to swing alone and (32) black boy sits on grass alone and (33) white man stands still with arms crossed looking out from under visor. (34) White woman returns with black man and bends to gather quilt and bag from grass. (35) White man in baseball cap holds small sleeping bag open while (36) young white woman puts baby in. (37) Young white woman orders black boy up off ground. (38) Black boy shakes head and stays on ground. (39) White woman slaps black boy, who (40) begins crying. (41) White woman carrying baby walks away with young black man and two girls while

(42) older white man follows, holding crying black boy by hand. (43) Family leaves playground and enters dusty road. (44) Family stops to wait for white man in baseball cap, who (45) returns slowly to park, picks up pair of child's thongs from grass, and (46) rejoins family. (47) Family walks on, heading toward marsh, short bridge, and red sky.

I am trying to learn that this playful man who teases me is the same as that serious man talking money to me so seriously he does not even see me anymore and that patient man offering me advice in times of trouble and that angry man slamming the door as he leaves the house. I have often wanted the playful man to be more serious, and the serious man to be less serious, and the patient man to be more playful. As for the angry man, he is a stranger to me and I do not feel it is wrong to hate him. Now I am learning that if I say bitter words to the angry man as he leaves the house, I am at the same time wounding the others, the ones I do not want to wound, the playful man teasing, the serious man talking money, and the patient man offering advice. Yet I look at the patient man, for instance, whom I would want above all to protect from such bitter words as mine, and though I tell myself he is the same man as the others, I can only believe I said those words, not to him, but to another, my enemy, who deserved all my anger.

Michel Butor says that to travel is to write, because to travel is to read. This can be developed further: To write is to travel, to write is to read, to read is to write, and to read is to travel. But George Steiner says that to translate is also to read, and to translate is to write, as to write is to translate and to read is to translate. So that we may say: To translate is to travel and to travel is to translate. To translate a travel writing, for example, is to read a travel writing, to write a travel writing, to read a writing, to write a writing, and to travel. But if because you are translating you read, and because writing translate, because traveling write, because traveling read, and because translating travel; that is, if to read is to translate, and to translate is to write, to write to travel, to read to travel, to write to read, to read to write, and to travel to translate; then to write is also to write, and to read is also to read, and even more, because when you read you read, but also travel, and because traveling read, therefore read and read; and when reading also write, therefore read; and reading also translate, therefore read; therefore read, read, read, and read. The same argument may be made for translating, traveling, and writing.

Gotheberg: Greatly Daring Dined

He was a good deal tossed and beaten about off the Skaw, before sailing up the river this morning. On board also were the Consul, Mr. Smith, and an iron merchant, Mr. Damm. Neither he nor his two servants have any common language with any inhabitant of the inn. Considerable parts of the town of Gotheberg were burned down, it being built almost entirely of wood, and they are rebuilding it with white brick.

He has completely satisfied his curiosity about the town.

On an excursion to Trolhatte, the harness breaks three or four times between every post. Here the traveler drives, and the peasant runs by the side of the carriage or gets up behind. He views with great interest the falls of Trolhatte. In an album at a small inn at Trolhatte, he inscribes some Greek anapests evoking his impressions of them.

He inspects the canal and the cataracts under the guidance of a fine old soldier. He sees several vessels loaded with iron and timber pass through the sluices. He receives great civilities from the English merchants, particularly from Mr. Smith, the Consul. He eats cheese and corn brandy, raw herrings and caviar, a joint, a roast, fish and soup, and can't help thinking of Pope's line, "greatly daring dined."

To Copenhagen: The Water, Merely Brackish

Leaving Gotheborg, he passes through country uncommonly dreary, destitute of wood, covered with sand or rock, then country that is well wooded and watered, bearing crops chiefly of rye or barley, with a few fields of wheat and occasional hop grounds. Many of the wood bridges are quite rotten and scarcely bear the weight of a carriage. Crossing the Sound after reaching Helsinborg, he sees with great surprise a flock of geese swimming in the sea, tastes the water, and finds it merely brackish.

His knowledge of Copenhagen is so far limited to the streets he has driven through and the walls of the room he is sitting in, but there is no appearance of poverty, none of the wooden houses of Sweden, and the people are well dressed. He has reason to be satisfied with his servants, particularly Poole, who is active and intelligent.

The Danish nobility have mostly retired to their country houses.

The Barren Province of Smolang

Leaving Helsinborg, he has traveled through extensive forests of fir and birch: this is the barren Province of Smolang, so thinly inhabited that in two days he met only one solitary traveler.

Poole has contrived to get on by composing a language of English, Dutch, German, Swedish, and Danish in which euphony is not the most predominant feature.

For some time he has got nothing to eat but some rye bread—much too hard, black, and sour, he thinks, for any human being to eat. He might have had plenty of some raw salt goose if he had liked.

Stockholm is not so regular as Copenhagen, but more magnificent.

He has been to the Arsenal and seen the skin of the horse that carried Gustavus Adolphus at the battle of Lutzen, and the clothes in which Charles XII was shot.

He has sent his father two pieces of Swedish money, which is so heavy that when it was used as current coin, a public officer receiving a quarter's allowance had to bring a cart to carry it away.

To Westeras

In Upsala he visited the Cathedral and found there a man who could speak Latin very fluently. The Rector Magnificus was not at home. He was detained some time in a forest of fir and birch by the axletree breaking. In general, he is annoyed by having to find separate lodgings for himself and his horses in each town.

His Swedish has made the most terrible havoc with the little German he knows.

In Abo

He understands there is a gloom over the Russian court.

St. Petersburg: Rubbers of Whist

The immense forests of fir strike the imagination at first but then become tedious from their excessive uniformity. He has eaten partridges and a cock of the woods. As he advances in Russian Finland he finds everything getting more and more Russian: the churches begin to be ornamented with gilt domes and the number of persons wearing beards continues to increase. A postmaster addresses him in Latin but in spite of that is not very civil. The roads are so bad that eight horses will not draw him along and he is helped up the mountain by some peasants. He sees two wolves. He crosses the Neva over a wooden bridge. He is amused at finding his old friends the Irish jaunting-cars.

The most striking objects here are certainly the common people.

He has a poor opinion of the honesty of the country when he finds in the Russian language a single word to express "the perversion of Justice by a Judge," as in

Arabic there is a word to express "a bribe offered to a Judge."

In the Russian language they have only one word to express the ideas of *red* and *beautiful*, as the Romans used the word "purple" without any reference to color, as for instance "purple snow."

He is bored by the society of the people of St. Petersburg, where he plays rubbers of whist without any amusing conversation. He considers card games even more dull and unentertaining than spitting over a bridge or tapping a tune with a walking stick on a pair of boots.

The general appearance of the city is magnificent, and he sees this as proof of what may be done with brick and plaster—though the surrounding country is very flat, dull, and marshy. The weather begins to be cold, and a stove within and a pelisse without doors are necessary.

He wishes to see the ice-hills and sledges, and the frozen markets.

He goes to a Russian tragedy in five acts by mistake, thinking it is a French opera. Yet he expects in course of time to be able to converse with his friends the Sclavonians. He sees the Tauride, now lapsed to the crown, behind which is a winter garden laid out in parterres and gravel walks, filled with orange trees and other exotics, and evenly heated by a great number of stoves. The Neva is now blocked by large pieces of ice

[88]

floating down from the Ladoga. Though the temperature has been down to twenty degrees Fahrenheit below freezing, that is not considered to be much at all here.

The Empress gives birth to an Archduchess. When the Court assembles to pay their respects, the person who most attracts attention is Prince Hypsilantes, the Hospodar of Wallachia, and the Greeks of his train.

There is not much variety in his mode of life. He studies Russian in the morning.

He begins to be very tired of this place and its inhabitants: their hospitality; the voracious gluttony on every side of him; their barefaced cheating; their conversation, with its miserable lack of information and ideas; their constant fear of Siberia; their coldness, dullness, and lack of energy. The Poles are infinitely the most gentlemanlike, and seem a superior order of men to their Russian masters.

He won't remain here as long as he had intended, but will purchase two sledge kibitkas, and other supplies, and depart, not for Moscow, but for Archangel.

He imagines there must be something curious in driving reindeer on the ice of the White Sea.

To Archangel: The Mayor Makes a Speech

He buys two sledges covered with a tilt, furnishes them with a mattress, and lays in frozen beefsteaks, Madeira, brandy, and a large saucepan. For the trip he dresses in flannel, over that his ordinary clothes, over his boots fur shoes, over the fur shoes a pair of fur boots, covers his head with a cap of blue Astrachan wool, wraps himself in a sable pelisse, and over it all throws a bear skin.

On the road there are no accommodations, so he sees inside the houses of the peasantry. The whole family lives in one room in suffocating heat and smell and with a number of cockroaches, which swarm in the wooden huts. The dirt is excessive. But the people are civil, hospitable, cheerful, and intelligent, though addicted to spirits, quarrelsome among themselves, and inclined to cheat. They are more like the common Irish than anyone else he has seen. Peter the Great has by no means succeeded in forcing them to abandon their beards.

In the cottage, people come to see him dine. Twenty or thirty women crowd around him, examining him and asking him questions.

He passes through Ladoga and Vitigra. Approaching Kargossol, he counts from a distance nineteen churches, most of which have five balloon-like domes, gilt, copper, or painted in the most gaudy colors, and thinks it must be a magnificent town, but the number of churches here almost equals the number of houses.

In Archangel the Archbishop speaks Latin very fluently, but does not know whether the Samoyeds of his diocese are Pagans or Christians.

His hostess is anxious to show that they, too, have fruit, and brings in some specimens preserved. Here they have in the woods a berry with a strong taste of turpentine.

The mayor comes in during the evening and makes a speech to him in Russian three quarters of an hour long.

The temperature in Archangel is fifty-one degrees below freezing, both his hands are frozen, and Pauwells has a foot frozen. He goes northeast of Archangel, procures three sledges and twelve reindeer, and sets out over the unbeaten snow in search of a horde of Samoyeds. He finds them exactly on the Arctic circle in an immense plain of snow surrounded by several hundred reindeer. They are Pagans.

Back in Archangel, the cold has increased, and he is forced to bake his Madeira in an oven to get at it, and to carve his meat with an axe. It is nearly seventy degrees below freezing, barely three points above the point of congelation of mercury.

Moscow Is Immense and Extraordinary

Moscow is immense and extraordinary, after a journey over the worst road he has ever traveled in his life through a forest which scarcely ever suffered any interruption but continued with dreary uniformity from one capital to another.

He begins to be able to read Russian fairly easily,

and speak it sufficiently. Poole has also picked up enough.

He sends his younger brother a Samoyed sledge and three reindeer cut out of the teeth of a sea horse by a peasant at Archangel.

The extent of Moscow is prodigious despite its small population because in no quarter of the city do the houses stand contiguous. The Kremlin is certainly the most striking quarter, and nearly thirty gilt domes give it a most peculiar appearance.

He is much interested by the passage of regiments composed of some of the wandering nations. One day there passed two thousand Bashkirs from the Oremburg frontiers on their lean desert horses, armed with lances and bows, some clothed in complete armor, some with the twisted coat of mail or hauberk, some with grotesque caps, others with iron helmets. These people are Mohammedans. Their chief is dressed in a scarlet caftan, their music is a species of flute which they place in the corner of their mouths, singing at the same time. They are almost always at war with the Kirghese.

A regiment of Calmucs passes through. Their features are scarcely human. They worship the Dalai Lama. He also sees a number of Kirghese of the lesser and middle hordes.

He continues his study of Russian, finds the language sonorous, but thinks it hardly repays anyone the trouble of learning it, because there are so few original authors—upon the introduction of literature it was found much easier to translate. The national epic poem, however, about the conquest of the Tartars of Casan, would be good if it weren't for the insufferable monotony of the meter.

Another Trip to Petersburg

Proceeding along the frozen river, the postilions missed their road, came to a soft place on the ice, and the horses broke through. The kibitka in which he lay could not be opened from the inside and the postilions paid no attention to him, being concerned only with trying to save their horses. One of them woke Poole in his sledge to request an axe. Poole saw the vehicle half-floating in the water and had just time to open the leather covering. He jumped out upon the ice with his writing desk and the carriage went down to the bottom. One horse drowned.

In Petersburg, the Carnival was taking place: theaters erected on the river, ice-hills, long processions of sledges, multitudes of people, and public masquerades given morning and evening.

In Moscow Again, He Plans the Continuation of His Tour

Now Moscow is very dull during the fast.

He plans to get a large boat, embark at Casan, and

float down the Volga to Astracan sitting on a sofa. He will reach the banks of the Caspian.

The carriages he will use have not a particle of iron in their whole composition.

There is a sect of Eunuchs who do this to themselves for the kingdom of heaven. They had at one time propagated their doctrines to such an extent that the government was forced to interfere, afraid of depopulation. It seized a number of them and sent them to the mines of Siberia.

He is preparing for his journey, and he will be accompanied as far as Astracan by an American of South Carolina, Mr. Poinsett, one of the few liberal and literary and gentlemanlike men he has seen emerge from the forests of the New World.

He has hired a Tartar interpreter, whom his valet de chambre is somewhat afraid of and calls "Monsieur le Tartare."

He is waiting for letters from Casan about the condition of the roads, but because it is spring and travel by both sledge and carriage is precarious, there is almost no communication between towns.

An edict has appeared forbidding conversation on political subjects.

In the Russian Empire, where perhaps of three men whom you meet, one comes from China, another from Persia, and the third from Lapland, you lose your ideas of distance.

Foreign newspapers are prohibited.

He has gone up to the top of a high tower at one in the morning to see the spectacle of Moscow with its hundreds of churches illuminated on Easter Eve.

Then he has been very surprised to see all the females of the family run up to him and cry out, "Christ is risen from the dead!"

When he sets out he and Mr. Poinsett will each be armed with a double-barreled gun, a brace of pistols, a dagger, and a Persian saber; each of the four servants also will have his pistols and cutlass. He will be sorry to leave Moscow.

Casan: No Man Could Suppose Himself to Be in Europe

The accommodations along the way are as they have been all over Muscovy: one room, in which you sleep with the whole family in the midst of a suffocating heat and smell; no furniture to be found but a bench and table, and an absolute dearth of provisions.

As he proceeds he finds the Tartars in the villages increasing in numbers, and the Russian fur cap giving way to the Mohammedan turban or the small embroidered coif of the Chinese.

He sleeps in the cottage of a Tcheremisse, with neither chimney nor window. The women have their petticoats only to the knee and braid their hair in long tresses, to which are tied a number of brass cylinders.

No man could suppose himself to be in Europe—
though by courtesy Casan is in Europe—when he con-
templates the Tartar fortifications, the singular archi-
tecture of the churches and shops, and the groups of
Tartars, Tcheremesses, Tchouasses, Bashkirs, and
Armenians.

An Armenian merchant promises to have a boat
ready in two or three days.

To the Quarantine Grounds Near the Astracan

The beauty of the scenery on the Volga is gratifying,
the right bank mountainous and well wooded. After
passing Tsauritzin, where both banks were in Asia,
there is nothing on either side but vast deserts of sand.

He sees great numbers of pelicans. Islands are white
with them. He sees prodigious quantities of eagles, too.
He and the others eat well on sterlet and its caviar.
The number of fish in the Volga is astounding. The
Russian peasants won't eat some of them for reasons
of superstition. For example, he had too much of a
sort of fish like the chad, and offered them to the boat's
crew, but they refused them, saying that the fish swam
round and round, and were insane, and if they ate
them they, too, would become insane.

There is some reason for refusing pigeons, too, and
also hares.

Samara is the winter home of a number of Calmouks. Only during the summer do they wander with

their flocks in the vast steppes on the Asiatic side and encamp in their circular tents of felt. The heat of the Steppe is suffocating. The blasts of wind during the summer immediately destroy the flocks exposed to them, which instantly rot. The Tartars and Calmouks make every species of laitage known in Europe and also ardent spirits they distill from cow's and mare's milk.

He comes upon a village as distinguished for the excessive cleanliness of the houses and the neatness of the gardens as the Russian habitations are for their dirt and filth.

The town of Astracan is inhabited by thirteen or fourteen different nations, each description of merchants in a separate caravanserai.

His next excursion before he proceeds to the northern provinces of Persia will be a short distance into the desert to the habitation of a Calmouk Prince. He wants to go hawking with his daughter the Princess, who with her pipe at her mouth hunts on the unbroken horses of the desert.

Solianka: Banners in the Wind

He is staying in a village inhabited exclusively by Tartars. He visits a Calmouk camp and enters the tent of the chief Lama. It is very neat and covered with white felt, the floor matted and strewn with rose leaves. The priest shows the idols and sacred books. He brings out the banner of silk painted with the twelve signs of the zodiac. Some banners are inscribed with prayers. These are placed at the door of the tent, in the wind: letting them flutter about is supposed to be equivalent to saying the prayers. The Lama orders tea: the leaves and stalks are pressed into a large square cake and this is boiled up with butter and salt in the Mongol manner. It forms a nauseous mixture, but he drinks it and then takes his leave, all the village coming out of their tents and going down with him to the waterside. At least a third of the men in the village are priests.

To the Tartar Prince: An Enormous Sturgeon

He proceeds through the desert, which extends to the foot of Mount Caucasus. How different it is from Archangel: terrible heat instead of terrible cold, a plain of sand instead of a plain of snow, herds of camels belonging to the Calmouks instead of flocks of reindeer.

The ground is so flat they have no trouble getting along in their kibitkas. But they are often fooled by the appearance of extensive ranges of hills on the horizons, which are actually merely small inequalities magnified by intervening vapors.

The careless servants lose most of the water they have brought along with them, and then they suffer from extreme thirst, for the pools are as salt as sea water: their bottoms and sides are covered with beautiful crystals exhaling a strong smell of violets.

The plants all taste of salt, the dews are salt, and even some milk he gets from a Tartar is brackish.

Then there are swarms of mosquitoes, and he can't even talk or eat without having a mouthful of them. Sleeping is out of the question.

They cross a river where the water comes up to the windows of the carriage, which floats. They cross a marsh four miles broad and three or four feet deep.

In Kizliar he sells his kibitka and sends his carriage back to Moscow. He will cross the rest of the desert on horseback.

They spend the night in an encampment of Tartars, who bring them sour mare's milk. Early in the morning they arrive at the residence of the Tartar Prince. The people of the village bring him an enormous sturgeon that is still alive and lay it at his feet.

In the courtyard he observes a man with long hair, contrary to custom.

Derbend: His Apparent Magnitude Is Directly as his Distance

He sets out for Derbend with an escort. The caravan is very oddly composed: he and his American companion, a Swiss, a Dutchman, a Mulatto, a Tartar of Rezan, a body of Lesgees for escort, two Jews, an envoy from one of the native Princes returning from Petersburg, and three Circassian girls whom one of the guides

has bought in the mountains and is taking to sell at
Baku.

In Derbend he has lodgings in the home of an absent
Persian. He is sent carpets and cushions and inundated
with fruits and pilaus. His apparent magnitude is directly as his distance: if he was a great man at Kizliar
with one orderly man to wait on him, here he is twice
as great, since he has two.

In the evening he rides out with Persian friends on
a white horse with its tail dyed scarlet. The Persians
amuse themselves trying to unhorse each other, while
he himself admires the view of the Caspian Sea, the
steep rock on which the town is situated, the gardens
surrounding it, and part of the chain of Caucasus rising
behind it.

Garden of the World

The Russian commandant has given him an escort
of Cossacks and Persians as far as the River Samoor to
point out the most fordable parts and help them over.

The merchant of women is still part of the group.
Now, because his girls attracted some attention in the
earlier part of the journey, he encloses them in great
sacks of felt, though the sun is burning hot.

It would be worthwhile for a traveler to enquire into
the traditions of a colony of Jews who live in the Da-
gestan near the Samoor. The groundwork of their lan-

guage is Hebrew, though apparently not intelligible to the Jews of other countries.

The country from the River Samoor to Baku is fit to be the garden of the world. The crops cultivated seem to be rice, maize, cotton, millet, and a kind of bearded wheat. From the woods come apples, pears, plums, pomegranates, quinces, and white mulberries often covered with pods of silk. Almost every bush and forest tree has a vine creeping up it covered with clusters of very tolerable grapes. The main draft animal is the buffalo, the antelope is the main wild animal, and the howls of the jackals in the mountains would have disturbed their rest if they hadn't been so tired.

A *Large Party of Persians*

They are met by a large party of Persians headed by two brothers, who beg them to turn back to visit the Khan of Cuba. They refuse, and one brother declares they will not go farther and must fight their passage through, which they prepare to do. Since they are better armed, they would have been able to go on unmolested, but the merchant of women begs them not to desert him or he will be ruined: they have stolen his horses and say they will put him to death if he does not sell his women at their price. The party of travelers threatens to complain to the Khan at Cuba and the Persians restore the horses.

They rest in the evening at a rock called Beshbarmak,

or "the five fingers," which is a great sea mark on the Caspian. From there to Baku is almost a desert with now and then a ruined caravanserai.

The day after he arrives, he receives a visit from Cassim Elfina Beg, the principal Persian of the place.

All the innumerable arches he has seen have been pointed.

The Famous Sources of Naphtha

General Gurieff, the commandant, has made a party for them to see the famous sources of naphtha, and with him and Beg and several other Persians they ride out to the principal wells. The strong smell is perceptible at a great distance and the ground about appears of the consistency of hardened pitch. One of the wells yields white naphtha; in all the others it is black, but very liquid.

The Everlasting Fire and the Fruits Thereabouts

He rides five miles farther to see the everlasting fire and the adoration of the Magi. For about two miles square, if the earth is turned up and fire applied, the vapor that escapes inflames and burns until extinguished by a violent storm. In this way the peasants calcine their lime.

In the center of this spot of ground is a square building enclosing a court. The building contains a number of cells with separate entrances. The arches of the doors are pointed, and over each is a tablet with an inscription, in characters unknown to him. In one of the cells is a small platform of clay with two pipes conveying the vapor, one of which is kept constantly burning. The inhabitant of the cell says he is a Parsee from Hindostan, the building was paid for by his countrymen, and a certain number of persons were sent from India and remained until relieved. When asked why they were sent, he answered: To venerate and adore that flame. In the center of the quadrangle is a tumulus, from an opening in which blazes out the eternal fire, surrounded by smaller spiracles of flame.

The fruits thereabout come spontaneously to perfection.

Across the Desert: A Large Panther

From Baku he sets off across the desert to Shamachee. After seventy versts they stop at a stream of water and scare up a large panther that escapes into the mountains. Early the next morning they come to old Baku, now in ruins, and in the evening to Shamachee. Here he sleeps in one of the cells of a ruined caravanserai. The poor peasants who live in the ruins have been ordered by Mustapha Khan to give the travelers provisions.

The Town of Fettag

The next day he travels over hills covered with fruit trees, down into a valley, and up a very steep mountain near the summit of which he enters the town of Fettag, residence of Mustapha the Khan of Shirvaun. The Khan lives entirely in tents and appears to be the most unpolished, ignorant, and stupid of any of the native Princes so far.

The Khan gives them a feast where the precepts of Mohammed are totally disregarded; at the conclusion, singing and dancing girls are introduced according to the Persian custom. The Khan makes them a present of horses, carpets, etc.

Fettag to Teflis: The Secretary Falls Ill

In the evening of the next day they come to a camp occupied by Azai Sultan, who is gleeful because he has won a fight over stolen cattle with some mountain people belonging to the next Sultan. The following day they are received by Giafar Kouli Khan, who gives him a long account of the way he beat the Shach's troops with an inferior number. There are puzzling things about his story but they ask no questions because it is dangerous to puzzle a potentate.

Two nights later he sleeps on the banks of the River Koor, the Cyrus of the ancients. On the road from Ganja to Teflis, his secretary Pauwells falls ill with a putrid fever. There is no cart to be procured and they are given false information that causes them to lie out for three nights exposed to the unwholesome dews of the Koor. They then reach a Cossack station, where they leave the secretary. They ride on to Teflis and send back a cart for him, but though he has medical attention he dies within four or five days.

In Teflis: One of the Best Cities

He is glad to be at Teflis, one of the best cities in this part of Asia. The baths are supplied by a fine natural warm spring. The women deserve their reputation for beauty. Those that are sold for slaves to the Mohammedans are those that are called Circassians, for the Circassians or Tcherkesses who are themselves Mohammedans seldom sell their children.

He has a letter of introduction to the Queen of Imiretia in her capital on the banks of the Phasis. She is in fact merely a nominal sovereign. She does not live in a cave, as he had been told, but receives them in her house, in a room fitted with sofas, ornamented with looking glasses, and hung round with pictures of the imperial family.

The climate here, however, is unwholesome, singularly prejudicial to strangers, and he and his companion Poinsett go to bed with violent attacks of fever. The other three servants are ill, too.

He decides that Ispahan can't any longer be considered the capital of Persia.

He learns that Count Gudovitch has obtained a victory near Cars over Yussuff Pacha.

He hears that there are rumors of peace between France and Russia; nobody knows if England is included.

With the Help of Some Bark: Over the Caucasus

As soon as he can sit a horse he takes leave of his Georgian friends, and rides out of the town. The snow and ice on Mount Caucasus, along with the help of some bark he gets from a Roman Catholic missionary, restore him to perfect health and strength as soon as he begins ascending the mountain.

The Caucasus is inhabited by about twenty nations, most of them speaking distinct languages, so that the inhabitants of one valley, insulated from the rest of the world, often can't make themselves understood if they cross the mountain.

They have purchased a tent and thus avoid stopping in towns where there is plague. On this side of the Russian frontier, it almost threatens to wipe out some of the Mohammedan nations. In some of the villages he passes, all the people have died, other villages are completely deserted, they scarcely see one man in the whole country and the few they see they carefully avoid.

Some people of the tribe of the Caftouras intend to

attack them but by mistake attack some Cossacks instead. One Cossack is left dead and one mortally wounded.

They make thirty-six versts to Kobia, pass by Kazbek, the highest part of the Caucasus, make twenty-eight versts in the rocky valley of Dagran, then leave the mountain and advance to the fortress of Vladi Caveass. They cross the little Cabarda entirely depopulated by the plague. On the road he sees the dead bodies of Cossacks and fragments of their lances strewn about.

Here in Mozdok, they are in quarantine.

Mozdok to Taman: Fevers

The ground has recently been overflowed by the Terek, his tent is not waterproof and the country is famous for fevers. He lies several days on the earth with a violent fever, surrounded by basins to catch the rain, which does not stop him from being drenched by it.

A change of situation and a thorough tanning of bark make him well again, but he is detained at Georgievsk by the illness of his fellow traveler.

They will go along the Cuban to Taman, the site of the Greek colony Phanagoria, and so over the Cimmerian Bosphorus to Kerch, the ancient Panticapaeum.

Taman: In the European Manner

At Stauropol he has a third fever that reduces him so low he cannot stand without fainting away. His optic nerves become so relaxed as to make him blind; with his right eye he can scarcely distinguish at night the flame of a candle. As he regains strength, his vision returns.

He recovers from the fever by using James's Powder in very large doses, but remains some time very deaf, subject to alarming palpitations of the heart, and so weak that he cannot stand long.

At Taman, they are detained some time by their interpreter falling ill. They are determined to wait there for his recovery, but he grows weaker rather than stronger, being housed in a damp lodging. Fellow traveler Poinsett suffers so severely from a bilious fever and becomes so weak they are very apprehensive for him, but then all rapidly regain strength, due to some light frost, to living in the European manner, and to the great attention of General Fanshaw, the Governor of the Crimea, who is an Englishman.

Back to Moscow: A Scotch Physician

They stop off in Kiev, the third city in Russia. Here the language is more Polish than Russian.

He loses another servant. The man is lethargic, re-fuses to exercise, secretly throws away his medicine, grows worse, is brought along lying on a bed in a kibitka toward the house of an English merchant, halfway there gets out, with the help of another servant gets in again, falls into a lethargic sleep, and on their arrival at the inn in Moscow is found dead.

Thus, of four servants who left this city with them, only one has returned, a stout Negro of Poinsett's, who has borne the climate better than any of them.

Of his wardrobe, all he has left now is one coat and a pair of pantaloons.

He hopes to sail directly from Petersburg to Harwich. In the meantime, here in Moscow, he has put himself under the direction of a Scotch physician, Dr. Keir, who prescribes absolute repose for the next four months and has ordered a course of bark and vitriolic acid, beef, mutton, and claret.

Improved Health: A Gentlemanlike Slimness

His health has improved quickly, he has lost every bad symptom: his dropsical legs have reduced to a gentlemanlike slimness, a fair round belly swelled and as hard as a board has shrunk to its former insignificance, and he is no longer annoyed by palpitations of the heart and pulsations of the head.

Within the past three days he has recovered his voice, which he had lost for two months. He is leading the life of a monk.

Poinsett leaves soon. Then he will set about writing a journal of the tour, though the mode of traveling during the first part of the journey, and the scarcity of chairs and tables, as well as the illness of the second part, have been very unfavorable to journalizing. In addition, the few notes he had taken were rendered illegible by crossing a torrent.

The End of the Tour: Shipwreck

He goes to Petersburg and finds his friends Colonel and Mrs. Pollen. Together they will go to Liebau in the Dutchy of Courland and try to sail to England by way of Sweden. He is suffering from the shock his constitution received in the south of Russia. He has frequent attacks of fever and ague and is nursed by the Colonel and his wife.

After three weeks in Liebau they engage a passage to Carlscrona on the ship *Agatha*, embarking on April 2. They sail, the weather is fine, the ice lies close about a mile from shore, they get through it at the rate of two miles an hour and are in clear water by 3 p.m. All that day and the next they have light breezes from the southeast. On the fourth, at about 2 p.m., they sight the Island of Oeland at a distance of eight or nine miles. It is blowing very hard: in an hour they get close in and see the ice about a mile from the shore.

Colonel Pollen wonders if they can anchor under Oeland, and another passenger, an English seaman by the name of Mr. Smith, thinks not, as the ice would drift off and cut the cables. The captain says he will stand on to the southward till eight o'clock, then return to the island, but at eight and at twelve he will not go back: now it blows a gale of wind from the westward with a very heavy sea. The vessel makes much water and the pumps are choked with ballast. The crew will bail very little; the water gains fast.

On the fifth they run the whole day before the wind. At noon on the sixth, Colonel Pollen wonders if the vessel can keep the sea. The English seaman says that unless the sailors make more efforts to bail she can't live long, since they already have three feet of water in the hold and it is gaining on them. The best way to save themselves is to steer for some port in Prussia. The Colonel agrees and tells the captain. The captain agrees and recommends Liebau, but the Colonel objects on account of the English seaman and a certain Mr. Renny, who have both escaped from Russia without passports. The captain agrees to go to Memel, but says he has never been there in his life: if the English seaman will take the ship in, he will give it over into his charge when they come to the bar. The seaman agrees because he knows the harbor perfectly well.

At two o'clock in the morning on the seventh they sight land to the southward about fifteen miles from Memel. They are close in to a lee shore because of the captain's ignorance and carelessness in running so far in the dark. They haul the ship to by the wind on the larboard tack, and at four o'clock get sight of Memel, which the captain takes for Liebau until he is told otherwise, when he is very surprised. Colonel Pollen and the other gentlemen come on deck and tell the captain to give the charge to the English seaman, which he does.

At six they come to the bar, the tide running very high, with two men at the helm. The passengers are pressing around the helm in a way that is dangerous to themselves and prevents the helmsmen from seeing ahead very well, so the English seaman asks them to go below. But now, unfortunately, the captain sees the sea breaking over the bar and becomes so frightened that he runs immediately to the helm and with the help of his people puts it hard-a-port. Though the English seaman strives against this, in ten minutes they are on the Southlands.

The third time the ship strikes, she grounds and fills with water. They are about a mile and a half from shore.

There is a small roundhouse on deck and Mrs. Pollen, Mrs. Barnes, her three children, two gentlemen, a man and a maidservant get into this to save themselves from the sea. Colonel Pollen and the English seaman begin to clear the boats out; the sailors will not help. They get the small one out and three sailors get

into it with the captain. Lord Royston, who is in a very
weak state of health, tries to follow them but the English seaman prevents him, telling him it is not safe.
When the captain hears this, he gets out. When the
boat leaves the ship's side it turns over and the three
men drown.

They begin to clear the large boat. It is lashed to
the deck by strong tackling to the ring-bolts. A sea
comes and forces away part of the tackling. The English
seaman calls to Colonel Pollen to jump out or the next
sea will carry her and them all away. They are scarcely
out of her when she is washed overboard. Now they
have no hope but in the mercy of Providence. At nine
o'clock they cut away the mast to ease the vessel, but
can see nothing of the lifeboat, which makes them very
uneasy, for the sea is tremendous, breaking right over
their heads, and it is so very cold that it is impossible
to hold fast by anything.

Colonel Pollen wonders if the roundhouse will stand
and is told it will, as long as the bottom of the vessel.

Colonel Pollen goes to the door of the roundhouse
and begs Mrs. Pollen not to stir from the roundhouse,
for the lifeboat will soon come. It is now about half
past nine but no boat is to be seen. The vessel is entirely
full of water except near the roundhouse. Mr. Renny
is soon washed overboard and after him, at about ten
o'clock, all within a few seas of each other, Colonel

Pollen, Mr. Baillie, and Mr. Becker, one sailor, Lord Royston's servant, Mrs. Barnes's servant, and Lord Royston himself.

An account of the catastrophe is published three years later in the *Gentleman's Magazine* by the English seaman, Mr. Smith.

THE OTHER

She changes this thing in the house to annoy the other, and the other is annoyed and changes it back, and she changes this other thing in the house to annoy the other, and the other is annoyed and changes it back, and then she tells all this the way it happens to some others and they think it is funny, but the other hears it and does not think it is funny, but can't change it back.

A FRIEND OF MINE

I am thinking about a friend of mine, how she is not
only what she believes she is, she is also what friends
believe her to be, and what her family believes her to
be, and even what she is in the eyes of chance ac-
quaintances and total strangers. About certain things,
her friends have one opinion and she has another. She
thinks, for instance, that she is overweight and not as
well educated as she should be, but her friends know
she is perfectly thin and better educated than most of
us. About other things she agrees, for instance that she
is amusing in company, likes to be on time, likes other
people to be on time, and is not orderly in her house-
keeping. Perhaps it must be true that the things about
which we all agree are part of what she really is, or
what she really would be if there were such a thing as
what she really is, because when I look for what she
really is, I find only contradictions everywhere: even
when she and her friends all agree about something,
this thing may not seem correct to a chance acquain-
tance, who may find her sullen in company or her
rooms very neat, for instance, and will not be entirely
wrong, since there are times when she is dull, and
times when she keeps a neat house, though they are

not the same times, for she will not be neat when she is feeling dull.

All this being true of my friend, it occurs to me that I must not know altogether what I am, either, and that others know certain things about me better than I do, though I think I ought to know all there is to know and I proceed as if I do. Even once I see this, however, I have no choice but to continue to proceed as if I know altogether what I am, though I may also try to guess, from time to time, just what it is that others know that I do not know.

In this condition: stirred not only by men but by women, fat and thin, naked and clothed; by teenagers and children in latency; by animals such as horses and dogs; by certain vegetables such as carrots, zucchinis, eggplants, and cucumbers; by fruits such as melons, grapefruits, and kiwis; by certain plant parts such as petals, sepals, stamens, and pistils; by the bare arm of a wooden chair, a round vase holding flowers, a little hot sunlight, a plate of pudding, a person entering a tunnel in the distance, a puddle of water, a hand alighting on a smooth stone, a hand alighting on a bare shoulder, a naked tree limb; by anything curved, bare, and shining, as the limb or bole of a tree; by any touch, as the touch of a stranger handling money; by anything round and freely hanging, as tassels on a curtain, chestnut burrs on a twig in spring, a wet tea bag on its string; by anything glowing, as a hot coal; anything soft or slow, as a cat rising from a chair; anything smooth and dry, as a stone, or warm and glistening; anything sliding, anything sliding back and forth; anything sliding in and out with an oiled surface, as certain machine parts; anything of a certain shape, like the state of Florida; anything pounding, anything stroking; anything bolt upright, anything horizontal and gaping, as a certain sea anemone; anything warm, anything wet, anything wet and red, anything turning red, as the sun at evening; anything wet and pink; anything long and straight with a blunt end, as a pestle; anything coming out of anything else, as a snail from its shell, as a snail's horns from its head; anything opening; any stream of water running, any stream running, any stream spurting, any stream spouting; any cry, any soft cry, any grunt; anything going into anything else, as a hand searching in a purse; anything clutching, anything grasping; anything rising, anything tightening or filling, as a sail; anything dripping, anything hardening, anything softening.

When he says, "Go away and don't come back," you
are hurt by the words even though you know he does
not mean what the words say, or rather you think he
probably means "Go away" because he is so angry at
you he does not want you anywhere near him right
now, but you are quite sure he does not want you to
stay away, he must want you to come back, either soon
or later, depending on how quickly he may grow less
angry during the time you are away, how he may
remember other less angry feelings he often has for
you which may soften his anger now. But though he
does mean "Go away," he does not mean it as much
as he means the anger that the words have in them,
as he also means the anger in the words "don't come
back." He means all the anger meant by someone who
says such words and means what the words say, that
you should not come back, ever, or rather he means
most of the anger meant by such a person, for if he
meant all the anger he would also mean what the words
themselves say, that you should not come back, ever.
But, being angry, if he were merely to say, "I'm very
angry at you," you would not be as hurt as you are,
or you would not be hurt at all, even though the degree
of anger, if it could be measured, might be exactly the

same. Or perhaps the degree of anger could not be the same. Or perhaps it could be the same but the anger would have to be of a different kind, a kind that could be shared as a problem, whereas this kind can be told only in these words he does not mean. So it is not the anger in these words that hurts you, but the fact that he chooses to say words to you that mean you should never come back, even though he does not mean what the words say, even though only the words themselves mean what they say.

We went to church a year ago on Easter Sunday because we had just moved to this town and wanted to feel part of the community. At that time we put our name on the church mailing list and now we receive its newsletter.

Every day, almost, we walk to the post office in the late afternoon and then around by the park and on to the hardware store or the library.

On our way from the playground to the library, we sometimes see Pastor Elaine in her yard, in her shorts, weeding around the phlox near the back door, which has a sign on it that reads "Pastor's Study." Now we learn from what she writes in the church newsletter that she has lost most of her newly planted tomatoes and eggplants to a "night creature" and is angry.

"I was furious!" she says. She is furious not only at the night creature but also at herself for her carelessness or forgetfulness, because the same thing happened to her last year. "Why had I forgotten it?" she asks.

There is a point to her story, a lesson she wants to teach us, which is that "it is our human condition which brings us back again and again to doing the things we would rather not be doing. We are far from perfection. I forget this at times and get so annoyed with myself."

We are often angry at ourselves, too, for such things as carelessness and forgetfulness, and things we feel are much worse.

Pastor Elaine uses the Bible to illustrate her lesson. "Paul put it so well," she says, before going on to quote from *Romans*: "I do not understand what I do; for I don't do what I would like to do, but instead I do what I hate. What an unhappy man I am. Who will rescue me from this body that is taking me to death?"

This seems too strong a reaction for the mistake Pastor Elaine has made in her garden, since she is not doing what she "hates" by setting plants in the ground without proper fencing, but we read closely what she has to say because it does describe exactly what we often do. We often do what we hate. We often tell ourselves what we would like to do, most importantly that we would like to be kind to our children, and gentle with them, and patient, and then we do not do what we would like to do, but what we hate; that is, we lose our patience suddenly and shout at them, or squeeze them, or shake them, or pound our fist on the table and frighten them. And we, too, do not understand why. Is it that we do not want to do what we so much believe we want to do?

We are sometimes aware that the ugly sounds coming from us may be overheard by the good family next door, whose younger son is an altar boy at what they call the BVM or the Perpetual. But this does not have the power to stop us.

We are not Christian but we have a Bible belonging to a church-going mother of ours, and although we are not believers, we think that if we read the same words believers read, we might also be comforted or learn something. The passage quoted by Pastor Elaine is a little different in our Bible. It begins: "For that which I do I know not: for what I would, that do I not; but what I hate, that do I. For to will is present with me; but how to perform that which is good I find not. For the good that I would I do not: but the evil which I would not, that I do."

This sounds quite like our situation, though what we do, we would not call evil but wrong. We will, we will with great determination, up in the privacy of our study, up in the bathroom, anywhere we are alone. But when it comes to performing what is good, sitting over lunch between our two children, who are not bad children, if the older one, bored, is teasing us and the younger one, tired, is fussing, our will is weak, in fact it is powerless. Then what does it mean to will, at all, if we can't perform? All that willing, upstairs, is for nothing. It seems that we are able to will only from a very shallow place and when we draw upon all the will in us it is quickly used up and there is nothing left.

Or something else, if not that, is wrong with the way we will.

When we lose our patience so suddenly, we feel possessed, as by some outside force, almost as it is described in the next lines we read: "Now if I do that I would not, it is no more I that do it, but sin that dwelleth in me. For I know that in me (that is, in my flesh), dwelleth no good thing." It is as though it were not we who were doing what we do, but some being we do not recognize. Certainly we do not recognize ourselves, in our fury, as what we have so lately been, gentle, for we can be gentle. Only, this other being does not seem like sin to us, but a living demon, and does not seem to dwell in us, but only to come into us sometimes and then leave again. Unless it is in us all the time, but quiet, and is then roused by some aggravation.

"I see another law in my members, warring against the law of my mind," says our Bible. But if there is another law in us, it does not seem to be in our members, in our body, but elsewhere, in our passions, raging like a storm, possessing us, and warring against the law of our mind. Unless, arising in our passions, it then spreads to our members, for we can sometimes feel that into our flesh no good thing comes: our blood becomes hot and our nerves sing, when we are angry.

A small italic *c* next to "in me (that is, in my flesh) dwelleth no good thing" refers us to two sentences in

Genesis and we look through the book for those sentences. The first one we find reads: "The imagination of man's heart is evil from his youth." The second uses many of the same words but does not mean exactly the same thing: "Every imagination of the thoughts of his heart was only evil continually." We will not say that we are filled with evil continually, because if no good thing comes into our flesh, it comes only sometimes. If we know it is not in us all the time, though, we may be able to say it is not just wrong but evil, this thing, this demon or poison that comes into us and pinches and wrinkles our features so that we are told, "You should see your face!"

"Who shall deliver me from the body of this death?" the passage continues. But in our case, we often become so ashamed that we wish we might be rescued right now, in the midst of life, from this body that is sometimes so filled with no good thing and so obedient to a law that wars against the law of our mind—our sharp mind, but our weak mind. Or our sharp mind, but our weak will. Or our strong will, but our disobedient will. Is that it—that our mind is sharp and has a law, but our will is strong and disobedient?

Toward the end of the newsletter we read that Pastor Elaine will be away for some weeks over the summer and that if we should need spiritual assistance during this time we may call any elder or the vice president, whose telephone number she gives. But in this town we would not be able to go to any elder or the vice president with our troubles.

If we were to go to Pastor Elaine herself for spiritual assistance, she might point to another passage, one we have seen by chance in Galatians: "But the fruit of the Spirit is love, joy, peace, longsuffering, gentleness, goodness, faith." How we would like to have in us this thing, the fruit of the Spirit. We read the list again and this time read it against the list of what is sometimes in us: love, joy, peace, gentleness, and goodness. We do not seem to have faith. As for long-suffering, we do not know if it is something one can have in small amounts. And now we see that it may be in the absence of long-suffering that no good thing comes into our flesh and we become vicious, as though possessed, and in the same moment lose, for a time, all love, joy, peace, gentleness, and goodness. Yet we do not know how to gain more long-suffering. It is not enough to want it, or to will it, or to will it from such a shallow place, anyway, as we do.

We take our usual walk to the post office and then by Pastor Elaine's house and on to the hardware store to look for a fluorescent light bulb. We see that Pastor Elaine has hung her wash on the line in back, above her phlox. We see through the window that the light is on in her study, although here, outside, the sun is bright. We think how we have been with our children this day or the day before, how we have stood holding the little one, so heavy, and put out our hand to push the arm of the older one to get him out of our way or to make him move faster, or driven in the car with them in the heat, damp, with a knot of rage in us, and yearned to reach inside, or outside, somewhere, and find more long-suffering, and have not known how to do it. And we wonder: What stores of anger have we laid down in the older one already? What hardness are we putting in the heart of the little one, where there was no hardness?

A man in our town is both a dog and its master. The master is impossibly unjust to the dog and makes its life a misery. One minute he wants to romp with it and the next minute he slaps it down for being so unruly. He beats it severely over its nose and hindquarters because it has slept on his bed and left its hairs on his pillow, and yet there are evenings when he is lonely and pulls the dog up to lie beside him, though the dog trembles with fear.

But the fault is not all on one side. No one else would tolerate a dog like this one. The smell of this dog is so sour and pungent that it is far more frightening and aggressive than the dog itself, who is shy and pees uncontrollably when taken by surprise. It is a foul and sopping creature.

Yet the master should hardly notice this, since he often drinks himself sick and spends the night curled against an alley wall.

At sundown we see him loping easily along the edge of the park, his nose to the breeze; he slows to a trot and circles to find a scent, scratches the stubble on his head and takes out a cigarette, lights it with trembling hands and then sits down on a bench after wiping it with his handkerchief. He smokes quietly until his cigarette has burned down to a stub. Then he explodes into wild anger and begins punching his head and kicking himself in the legs. When he is exhausted, he turns his face up to the sky and howls in frustration. Only sometimes, then, he will pet himself on the head until he is comforted.

If only I had a chance to learn from my mistakes, I would, but there are too many things you don't do twice; in fact, the most important things are things you don't do twice, so you can't do them better the second time. You do something wrong, and see what the right thing would have been, and are ready to do it, should you have the chance again, but the next experience is quite different, and your judgment is wrong again, and though you are now prepared for this experience should it repeat itself, you are not prepared for the next experience. If only, for instance, you could get married at eighteen twice, then the second time you could make sure you were not too young to do this, because you would have the perspective of being older, and would know that the person advising you to marry this man was giving you the wrong advice because his reasons were the same ones he gave you the last time he advised you to get married at eighteen. If you could bring a child from a first marriage into a second marriage a second time, you would know that generosity could turn to resentment if you did not do the right things and resentment back to kindness if you did, unless the man you married when you married a second time for the second time was quite different in temperament from the man you married when you married a second time for the first time, in which case you would have to marry that one twice also in order to learn just what the wisest course would be to take with a man of his temperament. If you could have your mother die a second time you might be prepared to fight for a private room that had no other person in it watching television while she died, but if you were prepared to fight for that, and did, you might have to lose your mother again in order to know enough to ask them to put her teeth in the right way and not the wrong way before you went into her room and saw her for the last time grinning so strangely, and then yet one more time to make sure her ashes were not buried again in that plain sort of airmail container in which she was sent north to the cemetery.

FEAR

Nearly every morning, a certain woman in our community comes running out of her house with her face white and her overcoat flapping wildly. She cries out, "Emergency, emergency," and one of us runs to her and holds her until her fears are calmed. We know she is making it up; nothing has really happened to her. But we understand, because there is hardly one of us who has not been moved at some time to do just what she has done, and every time, it has taken all our strength, and even the strength of our friends and families, too, to quiet us.

A certain woman had a very sharp consciousness but almost no memory. She remembered enough to get by from day to day. She remembered enough to work, and she worked hard. She did good work, and was paid for it, and earned enough to get by, but she did not remember her work, so that she could not answer questions about it, when people asked, as they did ask, since the work she did was interesting.

She remembered enough to get by, and to do her work, but she did not learn from what she did, or heard, or read. For she did read, she loved to read, and she took good notes on what she read, on the ideas that came to her from what she read, since she did have some ideas of her own, and even on her ideas about these ideas. Some of her ideas were even very good ideas, since she had a very sharp consciousness. And so she kept good notebooks and added to them year by year, and because many years passed this way, she had a long shelf of these notebooks, in which her handwriting became smaller and smaller.

Sometimes, when she was tired of reading a book, or when she was moved by a sudden curiosity she did not altogether understand, she would take an earlier notebook from the shelf and read a little of it, and she would be interested in what she read. She would be interested in the notes she had once taken on a book she was reading or on her own ideas. It would seem all new to her, and indeed most of it would be new to her. Sometimes she would only read and think, and sometimes she would make a note in her current notebook of what she was reading in a notebook from an earlier time, or she would make a note of an idea that came to her from what she was reading. Other times she would want to make a note but choose not to, since she did not think it quite right to make a note of what was already a note, though she did not fully understand what was not right about it. She wanted to make a note of a note she was reading, because this was her way of understanding what she read, though she was not assimilating what she read into her mind, or not for long, but only into another notebook. Or she wanted to make a note because to make a note was her way of thinking this thought.

Although most of what she read was new to her, sometimes she immediately recognized what she read and had no doubt that she herself had written it, and thought it. It seemed perfectly familiar to her, as though she had just thought it that very day, though in fact she had not thought it for some years, unless reading it again was the same as thinking it again, or the same as thinking it for the first time, and though she might never have thought it again, if she had not happened to read it in her notebook. And so she knew by this that these notebooks truly had a great deal to do with her, though it was hard for her to understand, and troubled her to try to understand, just how they had to do with her, how much they were of her and how much they were outside her and not of her, as they sat there on the shelf, being what she knew but did not know, being what she had read but did not remember reading, being what she had thought but did not now think, or remember thinking, or if she remembered, then did not know whether she was thinking it now or whether she had only once thought it, or understand why she had had a thought once and then years later the same thought, or a thought once and then never that same thought again.

Last fall my aunt burned to death when the boarding-house where she lived went up in flames. There was nothing left of her but a small pile of half-destroyed objects in one corner of her room, where I think she must have been sitting when the fire broke out: her false teeth, the frames of her glasses, her pearls, the eyelets of her leather boots, and her two long knitting needles coiled like snakes in the ash.

It was a gray day. Friends of the dead picked their way through the rubble like lonely ants, wheeling and backtracking. Every now and then a woman cried out in horror and was taken away. The chimneys were still intact: everything else had crumbled. Rain began to fall slowly on the crowd. Two firemen, pale from sleep-lessness, kicked the rubble with their boots and stopped several people from going near the house.

My aunt was dead. Or worse than dead, since there was nothing left of her to call dead. I wondered, with some fear, what would become of her old lover Mr. Knockly, a small man, who stood in the thickest cluster of men and women, his face like a white pimple among their overcoats, staring at the ruin as though his heart had been burnt out of him. When I went near him he ran away from me in his tiny boots. The collar of his jacket was turned up and his gray crew cut sparkled with rain. He moved as though he had been wounded in the legs and arms, the chest, the neck, as though he had been shot full of holes.

I saw him again on the following Sunday, at the funeral. In front of the church there were seven coffins. It occurred to me later that the coffins must have been empty. The church was full: only one of the dead had been a complete stranger—the police were still sending photographs of his teeth to cities as far away as Chicago. Near me sat an old man with glassy eyes who was drawn like a magnet to any gathering of people: I had once seen him throwing confetti onto a parade from the window of a deserted house. In the first pew was a pious woman who spent a great deal of time in church praying. Mr. Knockly was at the back, his head bowed so far over that it was barely visible.

He rode in the car with me behind the hearse, but looked out the window at the scrap-iron conversion plants and did not answer when I spoke to him. In the cemetery he stood by my aunt's coffin until it was lowered into the grave. His face was so palsied with grief, he seemed so nearly out of control, that I thought he would jump into the grave with her. But instead he turned away abruptly after the "dust to dust," and walked alone through the gate. There was no sign of him on the road when I returned in the car.

It was early October. The days were long and cool.

I went out every evening and walked. I would leave home before the sun set and stay out until night had fallen and the sky was completely dark. I went a different way each time, through back alleys, along dirt paths by the river, away from the river, over the hill on the outskirts of town, down through the main streets. I looked into doorways, into living rooms, into store windows; I watched through the glass as people ate dinner by themselves in coffee shops; I walked behind restaurants through clouds of steam from the kitchens and through the noise of clattering dishes.

I think I might have been searching for Mr. Knockly, though often I went where I was unlikely to find him. I didn't even know if he was still in town: with my aunt gone, there was no reason for him to stay here. But when I saw him again, I felt as though I had wanted, all this time, to see him again.

I was walking in the muddy lane behind a seafood restaurant, after a heavy rainstorm. The clouds had broken up and the sky was light in places, but the sun had set. I thought there was no one with me in the lane, but I heard a noise at the other end, and saw him. He was wearing a white work shirt and white apron with a red anchor on it, and he was emptying a small garbage pail into one of the large ones that stood in a row by the back door of the restaurant. As I went up to him, he was jerking the pail up and down

to free the clotted garbage. His head was bowed. I spoke
to him and he looked up quickly. Garbage spilled onto
the ground. He stood still for a moment; the emotion
that had been in his face at the funeral had died away:
his eyes, his mouth, were blunt and dogged. I said
something to him, and for a moment I thought he
would answer: his face moved, his lips unstuck. But
when I put out my hand to take hold of him, he shied
away and went indoors. There was a break in the noise
from the kitchen. I stood there sinking into the mud
and looking at the spilled garbage: crab's claws, sauce.
The door opened a crack, and a black face blocked the
light, then the door shut again. I felt uncomfortable.
I felt suddenly that it was very strange for me to be
there. I left.

But I went back the next evening, and the evening
after. The rest of the town had little meaning for me.
I would stop on the sidewalk in front of the restaurant,
pushed back and forth by the people passing behind
me, and stare at the red neon anchor in the window,
the tables inside, the cashier's desk, the waitresses, the
manager, and the assistant manager, with whom I had
once had some unpleasant dealings. I would catch
glimpses of Mr. Knockly through the swinging door at
the back. When someone noticed me, I would leave.
Or I would walk quickly through the lane behind,
almost afraid of being discovered there. I did this so
often that, even in the deepest silence, the noise of the

restaurant was in my ears, the sharp noise by the lane, the softer noise fronting the street.

I stayed out later and later in the evenings. I walked after the sky was completely dark, after I had seen people go home or into restaurants for dinner or into the movie house; sometimes I went on walking until the streets were deserted, the movie house darkened, and no one left in the restaurant but the owner sitting at one of the tables and writing something; and then I would not go home until the only waking life was in the bars along the riverfront. I explored every corner of the town: I thought there was not much in it that I liked, but there were things—a flight of steps, an arched doorway, the front of a factory—that drew me, and I would return to them again and again, look at them under different lights and in the dark, as if trying to discover something about them. The people of the town, though, remained strangers: I could not realize that I must be seeing some of them over and over again, it was as though each passed through only once, as though there were always new strangers coming here. And I felt so much a stranger myself that when, as rarely happened, I crossed the path of someone who knew me, and who spoke to me, I was startled and could hardly answer.

I expected to see Mr. Knockly again, but it did not occur to me to wait for him outside the restaurant. When I followed him, it was almost involuntary.

I was pushing my way through the crowd of people leaving work early in the evening when I saw his bowed shoulders and small head in front of me, moving more slowly than the people around him. I stopped, in order not to stumble over him. I watched him: he walked with his legs wide apart as if otherwise he might lose his balance, and he rocked slightly from side to side. I walked after him to the end of the main street. I dropped farther behind, and followed him in and out of the side streets. He circled back to the main street, more empty now, and then headed down to the river. There was no logic to the path he took. I was puzzled and tired. After an hour, night had fallen. We were not five minutes from where I had first seen him. Then he stopped short on the sidewalk. He stood still for a little while, then moved, then nearly ran, toward the river. I lost him.

The next night I waited for him outside the restaurant. I followed him again, and the same thing happened as had happened the night before, and for several nights after, the same. Always his brown coat ahead of me like a smudge in the gloom, always his pause and his sudden running, and always emptiness when I went after him. Then one night I did not lose him, but, running myself, followed him across the bridge and up to the door of a bar. I stopped there.

For a long while, I walked up and down the river trying to decide whether or not to go in and talk to

Mr. Knockly. I knew I had no business bothering him, and I was embarrassed. I leaned against a wall above the water, watching the wharf lights speckled on the surface: there was almost no current, but sometimes a slight breeze moved the water, and then the lights jumped. Below me, on the narrow and sodden strip of land, a woman, bulky in her coat, blacker than the black water, rummaged in a bag that stood at her feet, pulled things out of it that I couldn't identify in the dark, and threw them into the water. The soft splashes were the only noises, except for an occasional passing car up on the main street across the river, and an occasional shouting voice from over on the left somewhere beyond the warehouses.

At last I walked back to the bar. I don't know why I was so sure he would still be there. I went in and looked around the room. There were a few men standing over their drinks, watching me. Mr. Knockly was not one of them. I looked back into a smoky corner and saw two prostitutes sitting silently together. Their legs were crossed, their bare arms rested on the table in front of them. I went closer and saw that Mr. Knockly was there. He lay asleep with his head in the lap of one of them, his arms and legs tightly folded against his body, the tail of his overcoat in the sawdust on the floor. Then, as I stood there, the woman picked up her glass and emptied a little beer into his eyes, and into his ear. He hardly moved, only kicked the back of the bench with his foot. The women smiled slightly at him, looked away, looked up at me, and stared with hostility. I didn't know what to do, thought of buying a drink, but wasn't thirsty. I went out.

Weeks passed before I dared go to the back door of the seafood restaurant and ask for Mr. Knockly. A thin man of about forty, dressed in the same white shirt and apron that Mr. Knockly had worn, with pale arms, a dish towel over one shoulder and a stack of clean plates with red anchors on them in his hands, looked me up and down curiously. Other men in the kitchen also paused in their work. The man said that for weeks Mr. Knockly had not worked there. In a skeptical tone of voice he added that Mr. Knockly had found work somewhere else. He didn't know where.

For days after that, it rained. When the rain stopped, the wind sprang up, and when the wind abated, the rain came down again. I lost the sense of what clear daylight was. I had nearly given up hope of speaking to Mr. Knockly: I had thrown away the one reasonable chance. Then I saw him again late in the evening on the main street, in the rain. He was weaving back and forth over the sidewalk and jabbing the air with his fists. His hair had grown longer and was plastered to his forehead and cheeks. He plunged toward a woman who drew back against the wall in fright, he veered into the entrance of the movie house and out again, a tall man in a business suit caught him by the arms and pushed him aside, he stumbled over the curbstone and fell. As I went toward him, he picked himself up and rushed headlong into the alley beside the movie house. I went after him under the fire escapes. Though I had nearly caught up with him at the next corner, when I turned it the street was empty.

After that night, which was in late December, I was completely worn out. I did not walk as often, and when I walked did not see what was around me: though I looked up at the housefronts, at the sky, again and again I found myself watching the pavement that rolled out under my feet.

The days lengthened. In town, there was little sign of the changing season. I walked out into the country now and then, but though I tried to look, I saw nothing, or remembered nothing, of the spring. At the day's end I only felt, in the soles of my feet, the blanket of grass beyond the factories, the rutted road that skirted the woods, and the vibrating iron of the bridge over the narrow part of the river.

When Mr. Knockly died, I was there. Summer had come. I had walked in the morning, to the town dump. On the other side of the wire fence, among the hillocks of broken glass and old shoes, I saw a cluster of men bending over and flailing something with sticks and bottles. When I came up to the wire fence, they ran off over the rubble. I went through to Mr. Knockly. One arm was twisted under him. One temple was dented. His face was hidden in the ashes. I saw no blood.

On the far side of the dump, fires were blazing. The flames were barely visible in the sunlight. The meadows beyond trembled in the heat.

I telephoned the police and reported his murder. I hung up when they asked my name.

Often I think that his idea of what we should do is wrong, and my idea is right. Yet I know that he has often been right before, when I was wrong. And so I let him make his wrong decision, telling myself, though I can't believe it, that his wrong decision may actually be right. And then later it turns out, as it often has before, that his decision was the right one, after all. Or, rather, his decision was still wrong, but wrong for circumstances different from the circumstances as they actually were, while it was right for circumstances I clearly did not understand.

THE RAPE OF THE
TANUK WOMEN

One day when the Tanuk men were away from their village hunting, an entire village of Tunit men came to their igloos and raped their women to satisfy an old grudge. When the Tanuk men returned and saw the traces of blood and tears, they vowed to take revenge for this insult and immediately left for the village of the Tunit, several days' journey away over the thick coastal ice. They knew they would find the Tunit men sleeping as only men can sleep who have raped and traveled several days through the bitter winds of midwinter. Yet when they arrived in the Tunit village and crept through the passageways into the Tunit igloos, they found them cold and empty. They hacked off pieces of frozen meat from Tunit seal carcasses and chewed them as they deliberated upon their next move.

But in the absence of the Tanuk men, as the Tanuk women slowly recovered their calm, the Tunit men came creeping into their camp again and down the passageways into their igloos. Again the Tunit men lay with the Tanuk women and vanished into the vast stretches of sunless, icebound land that lay beyond the circle of igloos. While this was happening, however, the Tunit women returned to their camp and found the Tanuk men dozing there in frustration. Too disheartened to rape the Tunit women in revenge, as they might have done, the Tanuk men left them in order to search for the Tunit men elsewhere.

As they started toward home, Nigerk, the south wind, filled the air with snow and made it difficult for them to walk. They struggled on through the wall of dancing flakes, and suddenly before them they saw the shapes of men. They sprang with blood lust, thinking vengeance was within reach. Yet the shapes of men melted away at their touch and re-formed at a distance. Though the Tanuk men attacked them again and again, they could not harm them, for these were not the Tunit, as the Tanuk thought, but merely polar spirits.

Several days later, the Tanuk men reached their village and the igloos of their crazed wives and sisters. As their men had remained away, the women had been visited a third time by the Tunit and then, as though that were not injury enough, by the polar spirits as well, and they no longer recognized their own husbands and brothers. Their fear did not leave them until the sun rose in the spring. Only then, as the ice began to loosen its hold and the waters to reappear, did their eyes rest once again gently on their husbands and brothers.

These days I try to tell myself that what I feel is not very important. I've read this in several books now: what I feel is important but not the center of everything. Maybe I do see this, but I do not believe it deeply enough to act on it. I would like to believe it more deeply.

What a relief that would be. I wouldn't have to think about what I felt all the time, and try to control it, with all its complications and all its consequences. I wouldn't have to try to feel better all the time. In fact, if I didn't believe what I felt was so important, I probably wouldn't even feel so bad, and it wouldn't be so hard to feel better. I wouldn't have to say, Oh, I feel so awful, this is like the end for me here, in this dark living room late at night, with the dark street outside under the streetlights, I am so very alone, everyone else in the house asleep, there is no comfort anywhere, just me alone down here, I will never calm myself enough to sleep, never sleep, never be able to go on to the next day, I can't possibly go on, I can't live, even through the next minute.

If I believed that what I felt was not the center of everything, then it wouldn't be, but just one of many things, off to the side, and I would be able to see and pay attention to other things that were equally important, and in this way I would have some relief.

But it is curious how you can see that an idea is absolutely true and correct and yet not believe it deeply enough to act on it. So I still act as though my feelings were the center of everything, and they still cause me to end up alone by the living-room window late at night. What is different, now, is that I have this idea: I have the idea that soon I will no longer believe my feelings are the center of everything. This is a real comfort to me, because if you despair of going on, but at the same time tell yourself that your despair may not be very important, then either you stop despairing or you still despair but at the same time begin to see how your despair, too, might move off to the side, one of many things.

LOST THINGS

They are lost, but also not lost but somewhere in the world. Most of them are small, though two are larger, one a coat and one a dog. Of the small things, one is a valuable ring, one a valuable button. They are lost from me and where I am, but they are also not gone. They are somewhere else, and they are there to someone else, it may be. But if not there to someone else, the ring is, still, not lost to itself, but there, only not where I am, and the button, too, there, still, only not where I am.

I happened to write to my friend Mitch telling him what my life here was like and what I did all day. I told him that among other things I watched the Mary Tyler Moore Show every afternoon. I knew that he, unlike some people, would understand this. I have just gotten a letter back from him saying that I am not the only person he knows who watches it.

Mitch has a lot of odd pieces of information about people, both famous people and ordinary people. He is always reading books and newspapers, he has a very good memory and a lot of curiosity, and he is always talking to people, both friends and strangers. If he talks to a stranger, he likes to know where that person went to high school. If he talks to a friend, he often asks what that person had for lunch or dinner. He once told me that he tried to remember everything he learned from a conversation with a stranger in order to use it to begin or develop a conversation with another stranger. How suddenly talkative a stranger would become when he found that Mitch already knew a good deal about the politics of Buffalo, New York, for instance. He told me this as we were standing in front of an expensive boutique with a sidewalk display of purses on a busy avenue in the city. We were surrounded by strangers and he had just had a conversation with the man selling the purses.

At this time, which was a few years ago, before he and I both moved out of the city, he used to call me on the phone regularly and talk to me for as long as an hour if I was able to talk that long. I usually told him at some point in the conversation that I couldn't go on talking because I had to get back to work, and for that he would become annoyed with me. He wasn't working himself and spent a lot of time in his apartment reading, thinking, playing with his dog, and calling the few friends he stayed in touch with. I never saw his apartment. He told me it was filled with old paperback mysteries. He also borrowed books on a variety of subjects from the public library. He was the only person I knew, at that time, who used the public library. When he asked me what I had had for lunch or dinner, I was always surprised, but also pleased to tell him, probably because no one else was interested in what I had had for lunch or dinner.

In his letter Mitch says that he himself likes the show, and that Glenn Gould also liked it. I am terribly surprised by this. I see two of my worlds coming together that I had thought were as far apart as they could be.

This pianist was a model for me all the time I was a child growing up and learning to play the piano. I listened to certain of his records over and over and studied the jacket photographs of his handsome young face and thin shoulders and chest. Once out of my adolescence, I stopped studying his photographs with such attention but continued to imitate as best I could the clarity of his fingering, his peculiar ornamentation, and his interpretations of Bach in particular. I practiced the piano for as long as four hours at a time, sometimes six, beginning with scales and arpeggios and five-finger exercises, then working on one or two pieces, and then playing through whatever I liked from the books I had. I did not intend to make a career of music, but I could happily have spent my days working as hard at the piano as any professional, partly to avoid doing other things that were harder, but partly for the pleasure of it.

Now that my initial surprise has passed, I am pleased in several ways by the fact that he liked this show. For one thing, I now feel I have a companion watching the show with me, even though Glenn Gould is no longer alive. During his lifetime, he said several times that he would not play the piano after the age of fifty, and ten days after he turned fifty, he died of a stroke. This was a few years ago.

For another, the fact that this companion was so intelligent gives me a new respect for the show. Glenn Gould's standards were very high, at least concerning the composition and performance of music, and concerning his own writing. He was also articulate and opinionated, and wrote well about music and other subjects. He wrote about Schoenberg, Stokowski, Menuhin, Boulez, and he also wrote about musicians like Petula Clark. He said that when he was a student it had dismayed and puzzled him that any sane adult would include Mozart's pieces among the great musical treasures of the West, although he enjoyed playing them—he said he had instinctively disapproved of Alberti bases. He wrote about Toronto, television, and the idea of the north. He said that very few people who went into the north emerged unscathed: excited by the creative possibilities of the north, they tended to become philosophers of their own work. Rubenstein loved hotels, but Glenn Gould called himself a "motel man." He said that twice a year or so he would go along the north shore of Lake Superior where there were lumber and mining towns every fifty miles or so. He would stay in a motel and write for a few days. He said these towns had an extraordinary identity because they had grown up around one industry or one plant. He said that if he could arrange it, that would really be the sort of place in which he would like to spend his life.

Of course, it is also true, as I gradually discovered over the years, that he had many strange notions and habits. Schoenberg was one of his favorite composers, but Strauss was another. He was known to be a hypochondriac and excessively careful of his hands. He dressed warmly no matter what the season, and took his own folding chair with him to concerts, when he still gave concerts, sitting very low in relation to the keyboard. He sometimes practiced with the vacuum cleaner on because that way, he said, he could hear the skeleton of the music. Now Mitch tells me he was fond of a certain rather ugly female pop singer whom he taped, as he also taped this show I like so much. He called the singer's voice a "natural wonder," and was amazed by what she could do with it. Mitch does not explain what it was he liked about the television show, and I am still puzzling over this. His sense of humor must have had something to do with it—in his own writings he is quite funny.

Now that we live in a town where so many channels come in clearly, and I'm home alone with the baby so much, I watch the show almost every day. My husband has come to realize that I will always watch it when I can, and sometimes over dinner when we have nothing else to say to each other, he will ask about it. I will tell him something one of the characters said and I can see he is ready to laugh even before I tell it, though so often, in the case of other subjects, he is not terribly interested in what I say to him, especially when he sees that I am becoming enthusiastic.

He knows the characters because he used to watch the show when he lived alone in the city. When I lived alone in the city I watched it, too. It was on late at night, and there was a certain intimacy and intensity to watching it alone that way, with the darkness and quiet outside the windows. I watched with such concentration that I forgot everything else and entered the lives of those characters in that other city.

The intensity is gone now. In the late afternoon, the sun comes in the window almost horizontally across the living-room floor, there are wooden blocks everywhere on the rug, the baby is often playing beside me, I play with him to keep him busy, and I look up at the screen as often as I can. The baby is happy, and his noise, at the top of his voice, is often too loud for me to hear what the characters are saying, especially, it always seems, when they say something funny: there will be a remark that sets up the joke, the baby will yell over the next remark, and then there will be the laughter of the audience, so I know I've missed something that would probably have amused me, too, because the show is funny most of the time—it is well written and well acted and even on a bad day it has one or two truly funny moments. So I certainly can't forget where I am, or my own life.

Glenn Gould did not have children. He was not married. I don't know what he felt about women, even if I now know he liked the ugly singer and this show in which one woman is the central character and other women play important parts. I don't know whether he taped the show so that he wouldn't miss any of the episodes when he was away from the house performing, or, when that ended, recording, or for other reasons, or whether he taped it while he watched it, in order to build up a library of the series.

My routine with the baby is that I leave the house at about four o'clock, stop by the post office to pick up the mail, go on to the park, let the baby play for a while, go around by the hardware store or the library, and head home in time for the show, which starts at 5:30. The streets are broad and peaceful, which is one reason we moved here, and the trees are in full leaf now. In fact, the main reason we moved here was so that I could do just what I'm doing, walk with the baby around the back streets and to the stores and the park.

When I walked in the city there was always a great deal to look at, and I could walk a mile or two without noticing how far I had gone. Every building was different, every person was different. Every building had some kind of interesting detail on its cornice or above its windows and doorways, and the streets were so crowded that I passed another person every few seconds no matter what the time of day. Even the sky was more interesting there than it is here, because it spread out so softly behind and above the towers and the sharp upper edges of the buildings.

There is not much to look at in this town of bare and plain houses and yards, so I look hard at what there is, lawns, ornamental trees and foundation plantings, sometimes a very modest and carefully limited flower bed lining a front walk for a few yards or forming a small island in a lawn. I look at the shapes of the houses, the rooflines, the garages, trying to find something to think about. For instance, I will realize that a certain garage set back behind a house must once have been a small barn, with a horse and carriage in it and hay in the hayloft above.

Many of the houses are old, and must have had a henhouse out back, a fruit tree or two, a vegetable garden, and grapevines. Then little by little properties were neatened, shade trees and hedges were cut down, vines uprooted, trim removed from porches, porches removed from houses, and outbuildings dismantled. There are just a few interesting things to see: on a dead-end street, three disused greenhouses side by side with a "For Sale" sign in the grass in front of them; one slightly wild yard with a picket fence, overgrown shrubs and trees, and a fish pond; and a few old barns, though the oldest, once a livery stable, was set on fire by teenagers around Christmas and burned to the ground.

The only livestock in town is kept by a former prisoner of war and his wife, who have a small house and yard near the grocery store, a tall hedge in front tangled in vines and decorated with windblown trash from the street, a driveway deep in pine needles instead of asphalt. They keep ducks and geese in back, surrounded by several layers of high fencing that conceals them from the eyes of customers in the adjacent bank parking lot. Only on certain days in the warm weather do I remember the birds are there because the smell of manure hangs over the sidewalk, and then again on certain days in winter because the geese honk when it begins to snow.

If I go directly from the post office to the hardware store or the library without going to the park, I pass the Reformed Church and Pastor Elaine's house. It is a large house, though she lives alone. Stout tree roots have buckled the sidewalk next to it and the baby carriage jolts over that spot. At the hardware store, the two women in charge always speak kindly to the baby. They are both mothers, though their children are older and come into the store after school to do their homework and help out at the cash register. To reach the library I cross the street by the butcher shop, at the only traffic light in town. On the way back, I sometimes stop in at the grocery store to buy milk and bananas. I get home in time for the show, put the carriage on the back porch by the trumpet vine, take the baby into the living room, and settle on the floor with him.

He has changed in the months since I started watching the show here. Now he can stand up and is tall enough to reach over the edge of the table and touch the controls. The show does not change the same way, going forward chronologically, but jumps around in time. One day it jumped all the way back to the beginning of the series, to what appeared to be the first episode. I told my husband about it, but, maybe because I was excited and pleased, he was not very interested, and only shrugged.

Because the show jumps around in time, hairstyles are different every day, sometimes longer and flatter, sometimes shorter and more buoyant, sometimes so dated they look silly. Sometimes the fashions of the clothes are silly too, sometimes merely prim. When the clothes and hairstyles look silly, I feel sillier watching the show, and when they are closer to what I would wear myself, I feel less silly, though now, after what Mitch told me, I no longer feel embarrassed to be watching it.

At the end of the half hour I am sorry the show is over. I hunger for more. If I could, I would watch another half hour, and another, and another. I wish the baby would go to sleep and my husband would not come home for dinner. I want to stay in that other place, that other city that is a real city but one I have never visited. I want to go on looking through a window into someone else's life, someone else's office, someone else's apartment, a friend coming in the door, a friend staying for supper, usually salad, a woman tossing salad, always neatly dressed. There is order in that other world. Mary says that order is possible and, since she is gentle and kind if somewhat brittle, that kindness is possible, too. The friend who comes down from upstairs and stays for supper is not so tidy, and is not always kind, but sometimes selfish, so there is also room for human failing, and for a kind of recklessness or passion.

Another comedy follows this one, and now and then I try to watch it just in order to stay somewhere else for a while, but it is not well acted or well written, it is not funny, even the audience laughter sounds forced, and I can't believe it. Instead, I go into the kitchen and begin to prepare dinner, if the baby will not stop me by holding onto my legs.

I am still trying to understand just how Glenn Gould identified with the orderly woman and the passionate woman, just what sort of companionship he found with these two women and the other characters, if that's what it was. He was something of a recluse, by choice. He arranged his life as he wanted it, scheduled his outside appointments as it suited him, watched television when he needed to, and was able to be selfish without hurting anyone. He was a generous and considerate friend, but he didn't meet his friends in person very often because he believed that personal encounters were distracting and unnecessary. He said he could comprehend a person's essence better over the phone.

He had long conversations with his friends over the phone, always with a cup of tea in front of him. These conversations usually started at midnight, just before he went to work, since he slept through the day and worked through the night.

SMOKE

Hummingbirds make explosions in the dying white flowers—not only the white flowers are dying but old women are falling from branches everywhere—in smoking pits outside the city, other dead things, too, are burning—and what can be done? Few people know. Dogs have been lost in more than one place, and their owners do not love the countryside anymore. No—old women have fallen and lie with their cancerous cheeks among the roots of oak trees. Everywhere, everywhere. And the earth is sprouting things we do not dare look at. And the smoking pits have consumed other unnamable things, things we are glad to see go. The smoke, tall and thick as mountains, makes our landscape. There are no more mountains. Long ago they were gone, not even in the memory of our grandfathers. The cloud, low over our heads, is our sky. It has been a long age since anyone saw a sky, saw anything blue. The fog is our velvet, our armchair, our bed. The trees are purple in it. The candles of flowers are out now. The fog is soft, it has no claws, not yet. Our grandmothers' purple teeth crave. They crave things we would not even recognize anymore, though our grandmothers remember—they cry out at a bridge. Too many things to name are gone and we

are left with this clowning earth, these cynical trees—
shadows, all, of themselves. And we, too, are beyond
help. Some only are less cancerous than others, that
is all, some have more left, of their bones, of their
hair, of their organs. Who can find a way around the
smoking pits, the greedy oaks? Who can find a path to
take among the lost and dying dogs back to where the
hummingbirds, though mad, still explode the flowers,
flowers still though dying?

FROM BELOW,
AS A NEIGHBOR

If I were not me and overheard me from below, as a neighbor, talking to him, I would say to myself how glad I was not to be her, not to be sounding the way she is sounding, with a voice like her voice and an opinion like her opinion. But I cannot hear myself from below, as a neighbor, I cannot hear how I ought not to sound, I cannot be glad I am not her, as I would be if I could hear her. Then again, since I am her, I am not sorry to be here, up above, where I cannot hear her as a neighbor, where I cannot say to myself, as I would have to from below, how glad I am not to be her.

At the family gathering, the great-grandmothers were put out on the sun porch. But because of some problem with the children, at the same time as the brother-in-law had fallen into a drunken stupor, the great-grandmothers were forgotten by everyone for a very long time. When we opened the glass door, made our way through the rubber trees, and approached the sunlit old women, it was too late: their gnarled hands had grown into the wood of their cane handles, their lips had cleaved together into one membrane, their eyeballs had hardened and were immovably focused out on the chestnut grove where the children were flashing to and fro. Only old Agnes had a little life left in her, we could hear her breath sucking through her mouth, we could see her heart laboring beneath her silk dress, but even as we went to her she shuddered and was still.

ETHICS

"Do unto others as you would have others do unto you." I heard, on an interview program about ethics, that this concept underlies all systems of ethics. If you really do unto your neighbor as you would have him do unto you, you will be living according to a good system of ethics. At the time, I was pleased to learn of a simple rule that made such sense. But now, when I try to apply it literally to one person I know, it doesn't seem to work. One of his problems is that he has a lot of hostility toward certain other people and when I imagine how he would have them do unto him I can only think he would in fact want them to be hostile toward him, as he imagines they are, because he is already so very hostile toward them. He would also want them to be suspicious of him to the same degree that he is suspicious of them, and bitter about him as he is bitter about them, because his feelings against them are so strong that he needs the full strength of what he imagines to be their feelings against him in order to continue feeling what he wants to feel against them. So, really, he is already doing unto those certain others as he would have them do unto him, though in fact it occurs to me that at this point he is only having certain feelings about them and not doing anything to them, so he may still be quite within some system of ethics, unless to feel something toward someone is in fact to do something to that person.

THE HOUSE BEHIND

We live in the house behind and can't see the street: our back windows face the gray stone of the city wall and our front windows look across the courtyard into the kitchens and bathrooms of the front house. The apartments inside the front house are lofty and comfortable, while ours are cramped and graceless. In the front house, maids live in the neat little rooms on the top floor and look out upon the spires of St-Etienne, but under the eaves of our house, tiny cubicles open in darkness onto a dusty corridor and the students and poor bachelors who sleep in them share one toilet by the back stairwell. Many tenants in the front house are high civil servants, while the house behind is filled with shopkeepers, salesmen, retired post-office employees, and unmarried schoolteachers. Naturally, we can't really blame the people in the front house for their wealth, but we are oppressed by it: we feel the difference. Yet this is not enough to explain the ill will that has always existed between the two houses.

I often sit by my front window at dusk, staring up at the sky and listening to the sounds of the people across from me. As the hour passes, the pigeons settle over the dormers, the traffic choking the narrow street beyond thins out, and the televisions in various apartments fill the air with voices and the sounds of violence. Now and again, I hear the lid of a metal trash can clang below me in the courtyard, and I see a shadowy figure carry away an empty plastic pail into one of the houses.

The trash cans were always a source of embarrassment, but now the atmosphere has sharpened: the tenants from the house in front are afraid to empty their trash. They will not enter the courtyard if another tenant is already there. I see them silhouetted in the doorway of the front hall as they wait. When there is no one in the courtyard, they empty their pails and walk quickly back across the cobblestones, anxious not to be caught there alone. Some of the old women from the house in front go down together, in pairs.

The murder took place nearly a year ago. It was curiously gratuitous. The murderer was a respected married man from our building and the murdered woman was one of the few kind people in the front house; in fact, one of the few who would associate with the people of the house behind. M. Martin had no real reason to kill her. I can only think that he was maddened by frustration: for years he had wanted to live in the house in front, and it was becoming clear to him that he never would.

It was dusk. Shutters were closing. I was sitting by my window. I saw the two of them meet in the courtyard by the trash cans. It was probably something she

LYDIA DAVIS

said to him, something perfectly innocent and friendly yet which made him realize once again just how different he was from her and from everyone else in the front house. She never should have spoken to him—most of them don't speak to us.

He had just emptied his pail when she came out. There was something so graceful about her that although she was carrying a garbage pail, she looked regal. I suppose he noticed how even her pail—of the same ordinary yellow plastic as his—was brighter, and how the garbage inside was more vivid than his. He must have noticed, too, how fresh and clean her dress was, how it wafted gently around her strong and healthy legs, how sweet the smell was that rose from it, and how luminous her skin was in the fading daylight, how her eyes glimmered with the constant slightly frenetic look of happiness that she wore, and how her light hair glinted with silver and swelled under its pins. He had stooped over his pail and was scraping the inside of it with a blunt hunting knife when she came out, gliding over the cobblestones toward him.

It was so dark by then that only the whiteness of her dress would have been clearly visible to him at first. He remained silent—for, scrupulously polite, he was never the first to speak to a person from the front house—and quickly turned his eyes away from her. But not quickly enough, for she answered his look and spoke.

She probably said something casual about how soft the evening was. If she hadn't spoken, his fury might not have been unleashed by the gentle sound of her voice. But in that instant he must have realized that for him the evening could never be as soft as it was for her. Or else something in her tone—something too kind, something just condescending enough to make him see that he was doomed to remain where he was—pushed him out of control. He straightened like a shot, as though something in him had snapped, and in one motion drove his knife into her throat.

I saw it all from above. It happened very quickly and quietly. I did not do anything. For a while I did not even realize what I had seen: life is so uneventful back here that I have almost lost the ability to react. But there was also something arresting in the sight of it: he was a strong and well-made man, an experienced hunter, and she was as slight and graceful as a doe. His gesture was a classically beautiful one; and she slumped down onto the cobblestones as quietly as a mist melting away from the surface of a pond. Even when I was able to think, I did not do anything.

As I watched, several people came to the back door of the house in front and the front door of our own house and stopped short with their garbage pails when they saw her lying there and him standing motionless above her. His pail stood empty at his feet, scraped clean, the handle of her pail was still clenched in her hand, and her garbage had spilled over the stones beside her, which was, strangely, almost as shocking to us as the murder itself. More and more tenants gathered and watched from the doorways. Their lips were moving, but I could not hear them over the noise of the televisions on all sides of me.

I think the reason no one did anything right away was that the murder had taken place in a sort of no-man's-land. If it had happened in our house or in theirs, action would have been taken—slowly in our house, briskly in theirs. But, as it was, people were in doubt: those from the house in front hesitated to lower themselves so far as to get involved in this, and those from our house hesitated to presume so far. In the end it was the concierge who dealt with it. The body was removed by the coroner and M. Martin left with the police. After the crowd had dispersed, the concierge swept up the spilled garbage, washed down the cobblestones, and returned each pail to the apartment where it belonged.

For a day or two, the people of both houses were visibly shaken. Talk was heard in the halls: in our house, voices rose like wind in the trees before a storm; in theirs, rich confident syllables rapped out like machine-gun fire. Encounters between the tenants of the two houses were more violent: people from our house jerked away from the others, if we met them in the street, and something in our faces cut short their conversations when we came within earshot.

But then the halls grew quiet again, and for a while it seemed as though little had changed. Perhaps this incident had been so far beyond our understanding that it could not affect us, I thought. The only difference seemed to be a certain blank look on the faces of the people in my building, as though they had gone into shock. But gradually I began to realize that the incident had left a deeper impression. Mistrust filled the air, and uneasiness. The people of the house in front were afraid of us here behind, now, and there was no communication between us at all. By killing the woman from the house in front, M. Martin had killed something more: we lost the last traces of our self-respect before the people from the house in front, because we all assumed responsibility for the crime. Now there was no point in pretending any longer. Some, it is true, were unaffected and continued to wear the rags of their dignity proudly. But most of the people in the house behind changed.

A night nurse lived across the landing from me. Every morning when she came home from work, I would wake to hear her heavy iron key ring clatter against the wooden door of her apartment, her keys rattle in the keyholes. Late in the afternoon she would come out again and shuffle around the landing on little cloth pads, dusting the banisters. Now she sat behind her door listening to the radio and coughing gently. The older Lamartine sister, who used to keep her door open a crack and listen to conversations going on in the hallway—occasionally becoming so excited that she stuck her sharp nose in the crack and threw out a comment or two—was now no longer seen at all except on Sundays, when she went out to early-morning Mass with a blue veil thrown over her head. My neighbor on the second floor, Mme Bac, left her laundry out for days, in all weathers, until the sour smell of it rose to me where I sat. Many tenants no longer cleaned their doormats. People were ashamed of their clothes, and wore raincoats when they went out. A musty odor filled the hallways: delivery boys and insurance salesmen groped their way up and down the stairs looking uncomfortable. Worst of all, everyone became surly and mean: we stopped speaking to one another, told tales to outsiders, and left mud on each other's landings.

Curiously enough, many pairs of houses in the city suffer from bad relations like ours: there is usually an uneasy truce between the two houses until some incident explodes the situation and it begins deteriorating. The people in the front houses become locked in their cold dignity and the people in the back houses lose confidence, their faces gray with shame.

Recently I caught myself on the point of throwing

an apple core down into the courtyard, and I realized how much I had already fallen under the influence of the house behind. My windowpanes are dim and fine curlicues of dust line the edges of the baseboards. If I don't leave now, I will soon be incapable of making the effort. I must lease an apartment in another section of the city and pack up my things.

I know that when I go to say goodbye to my neighbors, with whom I once got along quite well, some will not open their doors and others will look at me as though they do not know me. But there will be a few who manage to summon up enough of their old spirit of defiance and aggressive pride to shake my hand and wish me luck.

The hopeless look in their eyes will make me feel ashamed of leaving. But there is no way I can help them. In any case, I suspect that after some years things will return to normal. Habit will cause the people here behind to resume their shabby tidiness, their caustic morning gossip against the people from the house in front, their thrift in small purchases, their decency where no risk is involved—and as the people in both houses move away and are replaced by strangers, the whole affair will slowly be absorbed and forgotten. The only victims, in the end, will be M. Martin's wife, M. Martin himself, and the gentle woman M. Martin killed.

THE OUTING

An outburst of anger near the road, a refusal to speak on the path, a silence in the pine woods, a silence across the old railroad bridge, an attempt to be friendly in the water, a refusal to end the argument on the flat stones, a cry of anger on the steep bank of dirt, a weeping among the bushes.

A POSITION AT
THE UNIVERSITY

I think I know what sort of person I am. But then I think, But this stranger will imagine me quite otherwise when he or she hears this or that to my credit, for instance that I have a position at the university: the fact that I have a position at the university will appear to mean that I must be the sort of person who has a position at the university. But then I have to admit, with surprise, that, after all, it is true that I have a position at the university. And if it is true, then perhaps I really am the sort of person you imagine when you hear that a person has a position at the university. But, on the other hand, I know I am not the sort of person I imagine when I hear that a person has a position at the university. Then I see what the problem is: when others describe me this way, they appear to describe me completely, whereas in fact they do not describe me completely, and a complete description of me would include truths that seem quite incompatible with the fact that I have a position at the university.

EXAMPLES OF CONFUSION

1

On my way home, late at night, I look in at a coffee shop through its plate-glass front. It is all orange, with many signs about, the countertops and stools bare because the shop is closed, and far back, in the mirror that lines the back wall, back the depth of the shop and the depth of the reflected shop, in the darkness of that mirror, which is or is not the darkness of the night behind me, of the street I'm walking in, where the darkened Borough Hall building with its cupola stands at my back, though invisible in the mirror, I see my white jacket fluttering past disembodied, moving quickly since it is late. I think how remote I am, if that is me. Then think how remote, at least, that fluttering white thing is, for being me.

2

I sit on the floor of the bathroom adjoining my hotel room. It is nearly dawn and I have had too much to drink, so that certain simple things surprise me deeply. Or they are not simple. The hotel is very quiet. I look at my bare feet on the tiles in front of me and think: Those are her feet. I stand up and look in the mirror and think: There she is. She's looking at you.

Then I understand and say to myself: You have to say *she* if it's outside you. If your foot is over there, it's there away from you, it's *her* foot. In the mirror, you see something like your face. It's *her* face.

3

I am filled that day with vile or evil feelings—ill will toward one I think I should love, ill will toward myself, and discouragement over the work I think I should be doing. I look out the window of my borrowed house, out the narrow window of the smallest room. Suddenly there it is, my own spirit: an old white dog with bowed legs and swaying head staring around the corner of the porch with one mad, cataract-filled eye.

4

In the brief power outage, I feel my own electricity has been cut off and I will not be able to think. I fear that the power outage may have erased not only the work I have done but also a part of my own memory.

5

Driving in the rain, I see a crumpled brown thing ahead in the middle of the road. I think it is an animal. I feel sadness for it and for all the animals I have been seeing in the road and by the edge of the road. When I come closer, I find that it is not an animal but a paper bag. Then there is a moment when my sadness from before is still there along with the paper bag, so that I appear to feel sadness for the paper bag.

6

I am cleaning the kitchen floor. I am afraid of making a certain phone call. Now it is nine o'clock and I am done cleaning the floor. If I hang up this dustpan, if I put away this bucket, then there will be nothing left between me and the phone call, just as in W.'s dream he was not afraid of his execution until they came to shave him, when there was nothing left between him and his execution.

I began hesitating at nine o'clock. I think it must be nearly nine-thirty. But when I look at the clock, I see that only five minutes have gone by: the length of time I feel passing is really only the immensity of my hesitation.

7

I am reading a sentence by a certain poet as I eat my carrot. Then, although I know I have read it, although I know my eyes have passed along it and I have heard the words in my ears, I am sure I haven't really *read* it. I may mean *understood* it. But I may mean *consumed* it: I haven't consumed it because I was already eating the carrot. The carrot was a line, too.

8

Late in the evening, I am confused by drink and by all the turns in the streets he has led me through, and now he has his arm around me and asks me if I know where I am, in the city. I do not know exactly. He takes me up a few flights of stairs and into a small apartment. It looks familiar to me. Any room can seem like a room remembered from a dream, as can any doorway into a second room, but I look at it longer and I know I have been here before. It was another month, another year, he was not here, someone else was here, I did not know him, and this was an apartment belonging to a stranger.

9

As I sit waiting at a restaurant table I see out of the corner of my eye again and again a little cat come up onto the white marble doorstep of the restaurant entryway and then, every time I look over, it is not a little cat I see but the shadow, cast by the streetlamp, of a branch of large midsummer leaves moving in the wind from the river.

10

I am expecting a phone call at ten o'clock. The phone rings at 9:40. I am upstairs. Because I was not expecting it, the ring is sharper and louder. I answer: it is not the person I was expecting, and so the voice is also sharper and louder.

Now it is ten o'clock. I go out onto the front porch. I think the phone may ring while I am out here. I come in, and the phone rings just after I come in. But again it is someone else, and later I will think it was not that person but the other, the one who was supposed to call.

11

There is his right leg over my right leg, my left leg over his right leg, his left arm under my back, my right arm around his head, his right arm across my chest, my left arm across his right arm, and my right hand stroking his right temple. Now it becomes difficult to tell what part of what body is actually mine and what part his.

I rub his head as it lies pressed against mine, and I hear the strands of his hair chafing against his skull as though it is my own hair chafing against my own skull, as though I now hear with his ears, and from inside his head.

12

I have decided to take a certain book with me when I go. I am tired and can't think how I will carry it, though it is a small book. I am reading it before I go, and I read: *The antique bracelet she gave me with dozens of flowers etched into the tarnished brass.* Now I think that when I go out I will be able to wear the book around my wrist.

13

Looking out through the window of the coffee shop, I watch for a friend to appear. She is late. I am afraid she will not find this place. Now, if the many people passing in the street are quite unlike my friend, I feel she is still far away, or truly lost. But if a woman passes who is like her, I think she is close and will appear at any moment; and the more women pass who resemble her, or the more they resemble her, the closer I think she is, and the more likely to appear.

14

I was an unlikely person to invite to this party, and no one is talking to me. I believe the invitation was for someone else.

All day the clock answers my questions about the time very well, and so, wondering what the title of that book was, I look at the face of the clock for an answer.

I so nearly missed the bus, I still believe I am not on it now.

Because it is almost the end of the day, I think it is almost the end of the week.

That was such a peculiar thing to say to me, I do not believe it was said to me.

Because that expert gave me helpful information about his subject, which is horticulture, I think I can ask his advice about another subject, which is family relations.

I had such trouble finding this place, I believe I did not find it. I am talking to the person I came here to meet, but I believe he is still alone, waiting for me.

15

The ceiling is so high the light fades up under the peak of the roof. It takes a long time to walk through. Dust is everywhere, an even coating of blond dust; around every corner, a rolling table with a drawing board on it, a paper pinned to the board. Around the next corner, and the next, a painting on a wall, half finished, and before it, on the floor, cans of paint, brushes across the cans, and pails of soapy water colored red or blue. Not all the cans of paint are dusty. Not all parts of the floor are dusty.

At first it seems clear that this place is not part of a dream, but a place one moves through in waking life. But rounding the last corner into the remotest part, where the dust lies thickest over the boxes of charcoal sticks from Paris, and a yellowed sheet of muslin over the window is torn symmetrically in two spots, showing a white sky through two small panes of dusty glass, a part of this place that seems to have been forgotten or abandoned, or at least lain undisturbed longer than the rest, one is not sure that this place is not a place in a dream, though whether it lies entirely in that dream or not is hard to say, and if only partly, how it lies at once in that dream and in this waking—whether one stands in this waking and looks through a doorway into that more dusty part, into that dream, or whether one walks from this waking around a corner into the part more thickly covered with dust, into the more filtered light of the dream, the light that comes in through the yellowed sheet.

THE RACE OF THE PATIENT

MOTORCYCLISTS

In this race, it is not the swiftest who wins, but the slowest. At first it would seem easy to be the slowest of the motorcyclists, but it is not easy, because it is not in the temperament of a motorcyclist to be slow or patient.

The machines line up at the start, each more impressively outfitted and costly than the next, with white leather seats and armrests, with mahogany inlays, with pairs of antlers on their prows. All these accessories make them so exciting that it is hard not to drive them very fast.

After the starting gun sounds, the racers fire their engines and move off with a great noise, yet gain only inches over the hot, dusty track, their great black boots waddling alongside to steady them. Novices open cans of beer and begin drinking, but seasoned riders know that if they drink they will become too impatient to continue the race. Instead, they listen to radios, watch small portable televisions, and read magazines and light books as they keep an even step going, neither fast enough to lose the race nor slow enough to come to a stop, for, according to the rules, the motorcycles must keep moving forward at all times.

On either side of the track are men called checkers,

watching to see that no one violates this rule. Almost always, especially in the case of a very skillful driver, the motion of the machine can be perceived only by watching the lowering forward edges of the tires settle into the dust and the back edges lift out of it. The checkers sit in directors' chairs, getting up every few minutes to move them along the track.

Though the finish line is only a hundred yards away, by the time the afternoon is half over, the great machines are still clustered together midway down the track. Now, one by one the novices grow impatient, gun their engines with a happy racket, and let their machines wrest them from the still dust of their companions with a whip-like motion that leaves their heads crooked back and their locks of magnificently greasy hair flying straight out behind. In a moment they have flown across the finish line and are out of the race, and in the grayer dust beyond, away from the spectators, and away from the dark, glinting, plodding group of more patient motorcyclists, they assume an air of superiority, though in fact, now that no one is looking at them anymore, they feel ashamed that they have not been able to last the race out.

The finish is always a photo finish. The winner is often a veteran, not only of races for the slow but also of races for the swift. It seems simple to him, now, to build a powerful motor, gauge the condition and lie of the track, size up his competitors, and harden himself to win a race for the swift. Far more difficult to train himself to patience, steel his nerves to the pace of the slug, the snail, so slow that by comparison the crab moves as a galloping horse and the butterfly a bolt of lightning. To inure himself to look about at the visible world with a wonderful potential for speed between his legs, and yet to advance so slowly that any change in position is almost imperceptible, and the world, too, is unchanging but for the light cast by the traveling sun, which itself seems, by the end of the slow day, to have been shot from a swift bow.

AFFINITY

We feel an affinity with a certain thinker because we agree with him; or because he shows us what we were already thinking; or because he shows us in a more articulate form what we were already thinking; or because he shows us what we were on the point of thinking; or what we would sooner or later have thought; or what we would have thought much later if we hadn't read it now; or what we would have been likely to think but never would have thought if we hadn't read it now; or what we would have liked to think but never would have thought if we hadn't read it now.

Acknowledgments

Grateful acknowledgment is made to the editors of the following publications, in which these stories first appeared: "Meat, My Husband" in *TriQuarterly* © 1993; "Jack in the Country" in *Infolio* (London) as "E.'s Mistake" © 1986, in *Ottotole* 1987; "Foucault and Pencil" in *City Lights Review* © 1987; "The Mice" in *Conjunctions* © 1995; "The Professor" in *Harper's* © 1992; "The Cedar Trees" in *Conjunctions* © 1992; "The Cats in the Prison Recreation Hall" in *Conjunctions* © 1992; "Wife One in Country" in *City Lights Review* © 1987; "The Fish Tank" in *Hodos* © 1990; "The Center of the Story" in *Grand Street* © 1989; "Love" in *Conjunctions* © 1992; "Our Kindness" in *New American Writing* © 1992; "A Natural Disaster" in *Conjunctions* © 1992; "Odd Behavior" in *Conjunctions* © 1995; "St. Martin" in *Grand Street* © 1996; "Agreement" in *Indiana Review* © 1988; "In the Garment District" in *New American Writing* © 1992; "Disagreement" in *Indiana Review* © 1988; "The Actors" in *Conjunctions* © 1991; "What Was Interesting" in *Parnassus* © 1989; "In the Everglades" in *SUN* as "Tourist in the Everglades" © 1983; "The Family" in *The World* © 1996; "Trying to Learn" in *Conjunctions* © 1991; "To Reiterate" in *Pequod* © 1986; "Lord Royston's Tour" in *Conjunctions* © 1990; "The Other" in *Annandale* © 1993; "A Friend of Mine" in *Avec* as "My Friend" © 1989; "This Condition" in *Salt Hill Journal* © 1997; "Go Away" in *Conjunctions* © 1989; "Pastor Elaine's Newsletter" in *Pequod* as "Pastor Arlene's Newsletter" © 1991; "A Second Chance" in *New American Writing* © 1992; "Fear" in *Conjunctions* © 1995; "Almost No Memory" in *Conjunctions* © 1988; "Mr. Knockly" in *Living Hand* © 1975; "How He Is Often Right" in *Conjunctions* © 1989; "The Rape of the Tanuk Women" in *Conjunctions* © 1992; "What I Feel" in *Conjunctions* © 1991; "Lost Things" in

Conjunctions © 1995; "Glenn Gould" in *Doubletake* © 1997; "From Below, as a Neighbor" in *Indiana Review* © 1988; "The Great-grandmothers" in *New American Writing* © 1992; "The House Behind" in *Antaeus* © 1991; "The Outing" in *Conjunctions* © 1995; "A Position at the University" in *The World* © 1996; "Examples of Confusion" in *Conjunctions* as "Confusions" © 1988; "The Race of the Patient Motorcyclists" in *Conjunctions* © 1988; "Affinity" in *The Quarterly* © 1992. "The Thirteenth Woman," "A Man in Our Town" (under the title "The Dog Man"), "Mr. Knockly," and "Smoke" previously appeared in the collection *The Thirteenth Woman and Other Stories*, Living Hand Editions, 1976. "In the Everglades" previously appeared in the collection *Story and Other Stories*, The Figures, 1983. "Lord Royston's Tour" was adapted from *The Remains of Viscount Royston: A Memoir of His Life* by the Rev. Henry Pepys, London, 1838.

The author would also like to thank the following for support during the period in which these stories were written: the Fund for Poetry, the Ingram Merrill Foundation, the National Endowment for the Arts, and the Mrs. Giles Whiting Foundation.

LYDIA DAVIS is the author of six books of fiction, including *Break It Down* and *The End of the Story.* Her stories have been translated into French, German, and Spanish and have appeared in numerous magazines and anthologies. She is also a noted translator, from the French, and is currently working on the first volume of Proust's *In Search of Lost Time.* Lydia Davis teaches at Bard College and lives in Port Ewen, New York.